TRANSFER!

The ride is never by choice

Jennifer Starr

ISBN-13: 9781234567890
ISBN-10: 1477123456

Cover design by: Art Painter
Library of Congress Control Number: 2018675309
Printed in the United States of America

CONTENTS

PART I

CHAPTER ONE

Today after recess, I returned to class a little bit late for only the second or at most third time this semester. I apologized profusely and complimented yesterday's history lesson as best as I could because I didn't remember much of it, but my teacher gave me a detention slip anyway-- on the worst possible day. Grandma was around, meaning that none of my usual excuses would work.

She won't even believe any believable reasons. Grandma wouldn't accept that I could have been vomiting in the bathroom even though you can't make yourself stop throwing up when a bell happens to ring. I've tried conjuring up emergencies, including medical ones. Grandma wouldn't care whether I was getting help for a teacher who passed out or rescuing a tiny preschooler who ran off the school perimeter. Even realistic excuses fail. She wouldn't be concerned if I couldn't move my legs to walk to class after doing 972 jumping jacks at recess to raise money for childhood cancer.

When Mom's around, a detention slip is no big deal. All I do is tell her that something needs to be signed for school and she gets all flustered, looks at her watch, and requests that I bring it to her immediately because she's so very busy. She doesn't even look at it.

Grandma, on the other hand, reads each and every word of what she signs. Since she's been a little out of whack lately (I'm not quite ready to declare my grandmother nuts), I attempted a creative excuse for the detention slip: Some kid dropped a bag of chips into a small puddle when two Canadian geese came along and found it. Each goose had closed its beak on one side of the bag; they were pulling and tugging at the bag of chips like "tug of war." They were standing right in front of the school door, so I was absolutely not going to pass them.

I reminded Grandma of the day when we had been taking a nature walk around a pond where geese were flocking. We must have gotten too close to the geese, for two or three of them had begun chasing us. Their long black beaks were opening and closing menacingly. They were stretching their bodies to their full height, almost at the level of my waist, and madly flapping their wings while honking loudly. In a flash, we had backed away, petrified, narrowly escaping bodily injury. I told Grandma that I was not going to risk being mutilated for life by some geese just to get to class on time.

I could have better dealt with Grandma's lunacy if I could have used it to my advantage to get detention slips past her. Instead, the Canadian geese excuse, my best one yet, failed (but at least my friends got a laugh). My punishment was the usual 250-word essay on a short story of her choice, meaning a story not the least bit interesting to a thirteen-year-old boy.

And I am still left dealing with Grandma's madness. I'm seriously considering locking Grandma in the kitchen to protect my own sanity. Grandma's perfectly fine when she's in the kitchen, but I can't say the same when she's not. The first incident scared me so badly that I couldn't sleep.

Like in horror movies, the hour was late, the house was dark, and rain was coming down hard with frequent bouts of thunder. Grandma was staying overnight, as she customarily does when Mom is out of town, reading by the light of a single lamp in the living room; the remainder of the room was quite dim. Dad was tinkering in the basement, probably oblivious to the rain. I was enjoying a video game in my room.

"Danny, Danny," Grandma called urgently. The house nearly shook from the last clap of thunder. Terrified, I ran to the living room.

Grandma was wildly gesticulating by the window facing the front of our house. "Dreadful, quite dreadful." That was Grandma's way of saying something was really bad.

"What is it, Grandma?" I tried to focus through the rain drops pelting the window pane.

Grandma rubbed her temples nervously.

"It's gone. I'll have to show you next time, Danny."

"Show me what, Grandma?"

"Yes, that is the issue, the what."

"Are we in any danger?"

As she told me no more, I returned to my room, imagining monsters, witches on brooms, or terrorists with black masks circling the house most of the night. Needless to say, I was afraid to close my eyes to go to sleep.

In the morning, the combination of the sight of my familiar room bathed in sunlight, chirping birds, and sounds of traffic greatly alleviated my fears.

A few days later, I was taking a shower. Like most normal people, I do not leave my clothes on when I shower, so when Grandma let out a blood-curdling scream of "Danny Lewis," I became unraveled by the bad timing. I left the water running, grabbed every towel in sight, and raced to save my grandmother's life.

Grandma's forehead was smashed against the front living room window pane. Had she fallen and hit her head on the window? I didn't even have my phone. No, I didn't think she was injured because she was able to move and speak, pointing and saying, "Look, look."

My heart was still racing since I was expecting to find a terrorist with a rifle pointing at Grandma. Reflexively, I pulled her away from the window for safety. "I'll take care of it, Grandma," I announced as bravely as I could, conscious of my compromised state of being wrapped in towels. I carefully peeked out the window from the side, only to see nothing at all.

Grandma returned to the window. "Next time, Danny."

"Next time what, Grandma?"

She didn't answer. I really should have asked, "Next time when?" Now I would be scared to sit on the toilet because maybe she'd call. Even worse, the next time she hollered was when I was on the phone with my friend Eric Bayne from my eighth-grade class.

"Gotta go," I cut off Eric mid-sentence. This time, instead of running at top speed, I jogged to Grandma. As usual, she was at the front window. There were no bullet holes, no monsters, no by-standers, and hardly any noise outside.

"Next time," said Grandma.

By now, I was thinking, *yeah, next time Grandma goes to the mental hospital.* Eric called back, pressing me about the incident, so I answered honestly, "Wish I knew what that was about."

Still feeling upset after getting off with Eric, I decided Grandma was in no danger and I was done playing her window game. Reverting to my normal sarcastic ways, I stood by the living room window, scheming to shout in a shrill, girly voice, "Grandma, Grandma, come quick." Instead, I opted to draw a large monster with sizable fangs on four pieces of white printing paper taped together and hang it on the front window.

I didn't need to wait long. Minutes later, Grandma entered the room. "What is the meaning of this foolishness?"

"I spotted the monster myself and drew his picture." I smiled smugly.

"Nonsense, Danny. We are dealing with a bus."

"A bus?" That's all I got. Why would Grandma scream on the top of her lungs about a bus? And I'm pretty sure I've seen a city bus go down our block, too, like last year when the main street was being repaved. Certainly nothing to get excited about.

At a distance, I observed Grandma bustling in the kitchen, wearing an apron to protect her clothes. Interestingly, I never note any spots on her apron or any spills on the counter. She's a prim and proper woman, silver hair always pulled neatly into a bun with fashionable, rose-framed glasses resting on her nose. Having worked as an English teacher, her speech is articulate. Overall, she thinks logically, helps me with my English papers, and gives me good advice. I watched her cooking and she seemed pretty normal, almost too normal except for this bus nonsense.

For about a week, I thought I had taken care of the issue, until I heard Grandma calling, "Come here."

Not again, I thought and shook my head in disgust. Grandma was standing at the window peering out intently, her forehead nearly pushing the screen.

Groaning, I put down my phone and stood up from the sofa. The living room was becoming darker as the sun was setting. I wouldn't be able to see outside clearly anyway.

"Quick, Danny."

Obediently, I rushed toward the open window and looked out. Grandma pointed down the block. I didn't see anything but shadows.

"The bus just pulled away," Grandma apologized.

"Figures," I mumbled, staring absently.

"Danny." I put my head down, hoping Grandma would end the subject of buses. She didn't. "A man wearing a business suit boarded the bus. I wonder what he did wrong. I think he came out of the townhouse with the sunflowers growing in the front lawn. Do you know him?"

Now Grandma's imagination was seeing people boarding the bus and she wanted me to identify them! The situation was rapidly deteriorating. Soon I would have to involve Dad since as her son he might know what to do. For lack of a better option, I played along.

"No, Grandma. I don't know the man who lives in the townhouse with the sunflowers. You said he's a businessman? He's probably away on business most of the time, so you haven't seen him before. But if you keep seeing his face in our window, maybe he jumps up and down when there is a

9

full moon."

Grandma did not look pleased by my remarks.

"Sorry, Grandma," I uttered, but I pursued the issue further. "Grandma, why can't I see the bus while you are always able to see it? You also kind of know when it's there."

"I called you as soon as I saw the bus, Danny. In fact, I told you to hurry."

"Even if I had run at top speed, I don't think I could have caught up with that bus. The driver seems to like to drive really fast. Hey, do you think we can try to wait for it at the bus stop? Then, I would be able to see it close up." I marveled at the brilliance of my question, but it backfired. Grandma made an angry facial expression.

"You are a foolish boy." Grandma abruptly turned and headed toward the kitchen.

I fiddled around on my phone, finding it difficult to focus on my racing game. Instead of driving cars, I was seeing buses

Another time, I was watching a horror movie in the living room, snacking on popcorn and anxious that extraterrestrial creatures were coming to attack an elementary school. I felt a poke on my shoulder and jumped off the couch, heart racing, scared of finding a creature behind

me. Instead, Grandma was trying to get my attention.

"Quick, Danny, the bus is going down the block..."

That was the final straw. I was progressively becoming more uneasy and needed to speak with my father. I shouldn't have to be the one to take Grandma to a shrink.

A call to Eric helped me pass the time. Eric nearly always gets me to laugh, especially when he mocks our classmate Troy (who deserves it for always trying to get attention).

"So Troy was bragging that he had walked by TV cameras in front of a drugstore in his neighborhood and was on the 5 o'clock news last night. Like the guy had no clue what was going on. I googled the news and found the clip of Troy waving. The news story was about kids shoplifting from the store and there was Troy right in front of the store, waving stupidly. Like he's so clueless."

I laughed and forgot about my anxiety for a while. Finally, Dad returned home from work. We ate dinner together as is customary when Grandma stays over to watch me while Mom is out of town.

Unfortunately, Mom is out of town on business at least twice a month for about three to four days. None of my friends understand what my mother does; I only slightly understand. She is an orthotist, designing all kinds of braces (not for teeth) and crazy devices for people to wear on their body. Presently, she is trying to sell some new kind of back support. I don't get it. My back would hurt more if I wrapped some hard piece around it. She says you can move comfortably in a brace. I disagree: You can't move at all! What's even worse are the great big boots that she sells for broken bones in the feet. I would rather take a chance and wear my gym shoes. Don't even get me started on the neck braces; you can't even bend your neck to see the food on your own plate.

The minute Mom returns home, she's out the door to exercise. Eventually, I find her at home making work calls. On a lucky day, she'll sit and talk with me in the living room for fifteen minutes. Never more. Beyond that, her cell phone is sure to ring.

"I'm going to retire to the bedroom," Grandma announced after washing the dinner plates.

Thank goodness, I thought, because I desperately needed to speak to my father alone about her. As soon as her door closed, I addressed Dad. "Did Grandma ever make up stories when you were young?"

Dad is a great listener. I felt better already just by voicing my concerns, but his answer surprised me. "No, Grandma doesn't have much of an imagination. She read me lots and lots of books and would discuss current events but not much else."

No wonder Dad is so intelligent. His mother

read him a lot of books and probably the boring kind. Dad works as an engineer. Like Mom's work, I only partially understand what he does. I plan on doing something normal that my kids will understand, like being a fireman or a detective but not a bus driver.

"Did Grandma ever talk about buses?" I persisted, trying to be more specific.

"Buses?" Dad looked perplexed.

Now I would be pressed to provide him with some details. "Did she ever mention people on your block getting on buses?"

"Sure. I guess she might have mentioned a neighbor or two taking a bus to work or something."

"No, no. Did Grandma mention people that you didn't know getting on buses?"

"How would I have known whether people whom I didn't know were taking buses or not? You're talking crazy."

That practical father of mine was not following my train of thought. "Did Grandma make up stories about people getting on buses and ask you their names and what they did wrong?"

Patiently, Dad answered me. "No, Grandma did not make up stories. I can't recall any at all, though my aunt, her sister, was a great storyteller. Can you explain to me why you keep repeating the same question in different ways, Danny?"

I finally blurted it out: "Dad, I think Grandma is going nuts. She keeps pointing out the window and talking about buses, like all the time. And the worst part is that she calls me when I'm in the shower or on the phone, and I'm afraid I'll be in the middle of wiping my bottom, and it's just too much for me."

"This is new information to me, Danny. I will most definitely keep an eye on Grandma and take care of her. You don't need to worry about anything." Dad hugged me.

Just to be sure, I searched the newspaper before school the next day for an article about a strange or missing businessman. Of course, no such story existed. At school, no one in my eighth-grade class discussed the topic either. My friend Sara lives closer to the townhouse with sunflowers than me. She thought an older woman who mainly kept to herself lived there.

After school, I promptly pulled out my algebra assignment to get it out of the way. The first answer came right to me. I had just touched the tip of my pencil to the paper, when I heard calling. "Danny, Danny Lewis. Come quickly." I was livid. I stormed over to the window. Before I even entered the room, I knew I'd find Grandma standing by the window.

"Did you see the bus going down the block?" Grandma was staring intently at my face, waiting for an answer.

Possibly, I saw a flicker of something turn the corner. Perhaps a car had turned. "A little bit I think," I answered to make Grandma happy and to maybe help put an end to the craziness. The corners of her mouth turned up slightly. Backfire. I was feeding into her foolishness. Hastily, I added, "Where do the people get off the bus?"

Grandma gave me an icy stare and walked away without responding. I returned to my homework. The algebra problems no longer made any sense to me. Fuming, I stomped into the kitchen. "Grandma, I don't want to hear about buses anymore. I can't concentrate on my homework. This is not fair to me."

"You must not make light of this, Danny," Grandma cautioned.

When Dad came home from work, he sprinted over to hug me and inquire about my day.

"Grandma is doing the bus stuff again, Dad," I complained.

"I'm on it," assured Dad.

Sure enough, Dad bombarded Grandma with question after question on topic after topic. No mention was made of the bus. Having no other recourse, he directly confronted her. "Mom, Danny is a bit too old for your bus game. He doesn't quite know how to tell you himself."

I felt like hiding under the table. Grandma looked at me before responding.

"Scott, you very well know that I don't have

patience for games and trivialities, and I certainly dislike fanciful notions. Time must be spent wisely." On that note, Grandma pushed her chair back and excused herself to wash the dishes.

At this point, Dad became even more confused about the matter. I decided to be proactive and dialed Eric to invite him over after school the next day. Grandma would think twice about calling both of us over to the window— or so I hoped.

During recess, Eric listened to my dilemma. He was fascinated by the notion of mysterious buses driving down the street, picking up people who were never seen before. Eric suggested I speak with our science teacher, Mrs. Gainer, a former nurse.

"Mrs. Gainer." I approached her hesitantly after eating my lunch. "My grandmother is talking funny, and I'm worried. I know you were a nurse, so maybe you could explain to me what's going on."

"Oh my. Is she speaking gibberish? It could be a stroke." Mrs. Gainer looked concerned.

"Not like that. Her words are clear. She's just talking about crazy things that can't be true."

"Does she forget people's names or get lost? She may have some form of dementia."

"Not that either." I paused, frustrated. Mrs.

Gainer did not understand what I meant. "She talks crazy about a certain subject only. Everything else is completely normal."

"Maybe she has a unique perspective or opinion on that subject. And not everybody's thought processes are the same, and many are quite complex or unlike any other. What is normal for one person may seem illogical or even crazy to another."

I had not expected to have to spell things out for her. "This is different. No one, I mean no one, talks about invisible buses driving around town like my grandmother does."

Finally, I got Mrs. Gainer to stop rambling and trying to justify Grandma's lunacy. She thought for a moment. "Unfortunately, what you are describing is not a medical issue like the kinds I dealt with at the hospital. Your grandmother may have a psychological issue. I believe the school counselor Dr. Phyllis would be more suitable to have a discussion with you and your family."

"Been there, done that," I interrupted. Mrs. Gainer was taken by surprise, so I explained. "When my mother began going out of town for work, I would misbehave a lot at school to get attention, so they made me talk to Dr. Phil."

"Phyllis, Dr. Phyllis," sternly corrected my teacher. "Be respectful."

"And she said I needed adult level help... more than she can provide at the school."

"Danny, you are exaggerating."

"Honest. She got angry because I said I had one and a half parents. Biologically, I have two, but physically my mother is around only half of the time. Simple math from my perspective. Frankly, I'd rather talk to Dr. Seuss. He'd understand. Remember the line, 'Where is Brown? Mr. Brown is out of town.' Just like my mom."

Mrs. Gainer stifled a laugh. I bet she agreed with Dr. Phil about me needing the professional level stuff. The school bell thankfully ended the discussion.

Eric walked home with me after school. Grandma greeted us at the door. I don't remember what she said because I was anxious that she might do something crazier than point out the window. Grandma served home-made chocolate chip cookies; Eric and I talked baseball. I began to relax.

We ate and excused ourselves. "Thank you, Grandma," I said. "Thank you, Grandma," Eric repeated."

"What time does the bus arrive?" Eric whispered to me.

"Hopefully, the bus will have a flat tire today," I quipped.

In the middle of our video game, Grandma

entered the living room. Eric abruptly looked at her. "Any buses today, Grandma?"

I became embarrassed, breaking out in a sweat. I shot Eric a dirty look.

"None on this block," Grandma answered matter-of-factly, glancing out the window. She returned to the kitchen.

"Let's go down the block and talk to the people in the townhouse," suggested Eric. "Maybe we can find out the real story."

"Fine." I needed some air. At least Eric didn't judge me because of my looney grandmother. In fact, he was enjoying engaging in this bus game.

We found the townhouse with sunflowers in the front lawn and knocked lightly. A crotchety old lady flung open the door.

"What do you want?" she spoke gruffly.

Eric took the lead. "We haven't seen the guy in the business suit around lately and we...uh...we were concerned...yeah, worried about him."

I nodded eagerly in agreement.

"You haven't seen him because he's dead."

We hadn't expected that response, and our mouths hung open.

The older woman continued, "Bit the dust. In the ground. Six feet under."

My eyes met Eric's in utter disbelief. The woman kept going.

"Dead as a doorknob. Met his maker."

"Sorry. Really sorry," we apologized sincerely. Amazingly, the woman didn't look the least bit upset. Having no other words, we took our leave and scurried away.

"Poor excuse for a human being," the woman kept rambling.

Back home, I dared to ask Grandma another question. "Grandma, what kinds of people ride those buses?"

"The ride is never by choice."

Eric smirked. "Could the bus come for me?"

"If warranted." Grandma answered almost threateningly and hustled to the oven as a timer went off in the kitchen.

Warranted. A big word from a former English teacher that provided absolutely no clarity to the situation and made me feel even more uneasy.

"You know what that means? Hogwash," Eric offered. "Your grandmother is purposely being evasive. Let's just forget about the bus thing for today."

I hastily agreed. While Eric picked through some gadgets on my desk, my mind wandered back to the bus. Eric snapped his fingers at my blank stare. The bus thing completely left my mind.

CHAPTER TWO

As we finished dinner, Mom charged through the front door, having returned from her business trip. "How are you my sensational son?" She hugged me tightly.

I disliked her adjectives. I felt like I was some horribly uncomfortable item she was trying her best to sell. "Try these sensational foot orthotics (that feel good if you pretend that they are not in your shoes). Try this wonderful back brace (the plastic is so hard but at least you'll still be able to breathe)." I've heard her use all those kinds of words to customers on the telephone: sensational, outstanding, practical, effective, economical. Otherwise, people would run away from her products. I was not merchandise. Nevertheless, I remained respectful and polite. "How was your trip, Mom?"

"Good. Many sales. But I was on the plane and at the airport most of the day, so I would like to make it to the gym before bed. Got a bright and early meeting in the morning."

"Bet you do." I faintly smiled.

"Am I chopped liver?" Dad spoke in a cheerful tone, but I caught him lower his eyelids in disdain for just a fraction of a second.

"My magnificent husband, I missed you terribly." Mom pecked my father's cheek. She chatted with him for a moment or two and then was off to the gym.

Grandma snorted as the front door closed behind Mom. Dad picked up Grandma's overnight bags and drove her home. I restrained myself from asking Dad why Grandma was leaving when Mom had barely entered the house.

The house was quiet; I was all alone. I checked the locks on the front door to be sure no one could enter. For a few minutes, I loitered by the window. Not much was moving outside in the dark except for a taxi that rolled down the street. As my face was nearly completely rotated away from the window, something caught my eye. Whirling back around, I glimpsed a hazy, gray bus speeding by. I blinked and it was gone!

Instantly, I dialed Eric. "Eric, you won't believe it. I saw the bus!"

"It's in your imagination, Danny. Your grandmother is getting in your head."

The call was brief. Eric was probably right. Looking out the window again, everything appeared normal outside. The image of the bus had been so hazy. It must have been in my imagination after all. Nonetheless, I remained on the sofa in the living room until Dad returned, not wishing to be alone in my room in the back part of the house.

A knock at the door. I jumped. Dad could

not have returned home that soon, as Grandma's house was a few miles away. Keys in the lock. Mom entered.

"Oh, it's you." I sighed in relief.

"Gym closed early for maintenance," Mom explained in the most sorrowful of voices.

"Bad break." I couldn't muster any sympathy.

Mom stood still, bewildered, lost, unable to function. Then she smiled. Her behavior was most bizarre. What had happened?

"I know what to do! I can do an exercise video on the computer."

"Oh, yay." I faked excitement.

Mom didn't even notice my reaction. She was already on the way to her room. A few minutes later, I heard shuffling, jumping, and creaking of floor boards. I bet I could down a beer right now and she wouldn't be the wiser.

Finally, Dad returned home from dropping off Grandma. He genuinely beamed at my sight. "Everything OK?"

"Great." At seeing Dad, the hazy image of the bus became nearly indiscernible in my memory.

"Where's your mother? Wait. I think I feel the floor vibrating. Problem at the gym?"

"Something like that. I forgot what she said."

"Don't worry about it. Want some hot chocolate?"

By the time the water boiled for the hot chocolates, my mind was focused entirely on our baseball discussion. Mom emerged with a towel wrapped around her wet hair, having showered after exercise. "My perfect Danny, how are you?"

"Dad knows more about baseball than he used to. I'm teaching him all kinds of stuff..."

"Great," Mom interrupted my sentence. "Scott, honey, could you sweep the house? I need to set up some appointments for tomorrow."

"I was hoping to go down to the basement to relax and tinker a bit before retiring for the night. I've been busy keeping house and shopping while you were out of town, you know."

"Can you please just do me this small little favor? I'd really appreciate it." Mom didn't wait for an answer, walking away while busily scrolling on her phone.

Dad's face expressed utter disappointment. I felt so sorry for him. It was true that he hadn't had any time for himself the last few days.

"I'll sweep for you, Dad," I offered.

"I'll make it up to you, Danny." Dad always kept his promises.

Sure enough, a ten dollar bill was on my pillow at bedtime. I ran down to the basement to thank him and wish him a good night. He was happily tinkering with his tools. Next, I found Mom in the den, otherwise known as "Mom's office." She blew me kisses, intently listening to someone speaking to her on her cell phone. I was disappointed. Couldn't she spare five minutes to speak to her son before bedtime? After all, she had only returned home this very night.

The following day, I went to school feeling quite upset. Mom had left a note on the kitchen table: "Early morning meeting...love you." Dad prepared scrambled eggs and toast for me as best as he could. I pushed aside the brown parts of the eggs and picked at the yellow pieces.

The day further deteriorated. My English teacher, Mrs. Ellis, had previously assigned a letter to be written to an important person each student would like to meet. Predictably, some of the students wrote to the president, most others to famous actors and musicians. A creative student wrote to an FBI agent. One girl wrote to a famous author. Sara Swan from down my block addressed her dead grandfather to meet him in heaven. I had written to my own mother. The teacher called us to the front of the classroom one by one to read our letters aloud. I had not anticipated reading my letter in public, especially not in front of my classmates. I also had written the letter in a sarcastic tone after my mother had run out in the middle of one of our conversations--or at least my attempt at one. If my own mother doesn't have time to speak with me, why would I bother arranging to meet with someone important who has even less time?

My turn came; my face turned red. My friends would not understand, and Mrs. Ellis denied my request to pass.

Dear Mom,

When you are out of town, I learned that you are inaccessible during the day due to business obligations. You have explained to me that it is essential to maximize your time to meet with the largest number of clients. At night, you prepare for the following day.

When you are in town, I can't have a conversation with you when you are away at the gym. Even in the house, you often close your door and jump around your room. The remainder of your time seems to be consumed by telephone calls. (Grandma had suggested the word consumed.)

A school assignment helped me formulate an idea to resolve this issue. May I suggest arranging a meeting time with you as your clients do? We would then be able to have a meaningful conversation, and I could fill you in on all the details of my baseball games and school activities without being interrupted. I'd really like that.

My fellow classmates began laughing hysterically. Mrs. Ellis was not pleased, opening and closing her mouth a couple of times, obviously clueless what to say or how to handle the situation. Finally, she ordered me into Dr. Phyllis's office, causing even more ruckus and jeering.

"Dr. Phil will help Danny find his Mommy."

"Danny misses his Mommy. Maybe he needs a bottle."

Troy was spouting off to another guy, "Once I had to walk Danny home from school because his mother didn't come to pick him up."

I became livid, tightening my hands into fists. Eric's face lit up, and I relaxed my fingers, understanding Eric would not pass this opportunity to threaten the guy he detested for constantly spinning tall tales.

Eric had even made up a poem about Troy:

Troy, Troy, he acts like a little boy
He makes up stuff because he's not tough
Tries to deny when caught in a lie
And at school, he's the number one fool

Eric did come to my rescue, placing Troy in a choke hold. "At least Danny still has his head on. When I'm done with you, you will have nothing left up there."

Soon the two were rolling and wrestling on the floor. Two others joined the brawl. A fifth guy's foot was jerked, causing him to slide out of his seat onto the floor. The girls threw paper balls and erasers at the boys for good measure.

Meanwhile, Mrs. Ellis again failed to produce language. She dialed on her phone. Ancillary staff rushed in, and the fight was broken. Most of the boys were sent to the principal's office for certain detention. While I was directed to Dr. Phyllis,

I mouthed a quick "Thanks, man" to Eric, passing him at the door of the principal's office.

"Unfortunately, I cannot get a hold of your mother," apologized Dr. Phyllis.

"No worries." I was not the least surprised.

"No, Danny. I want to have a meeting with you and your mother right away."

"Good luck," I mumbled.

"Anything you want to talk about, Danny?"

"Yeah, what I'm doing in here. I'm not crazy, but I'd be happy to point out which kids in class have problems to make it easier for you if you want."

Dr. Phyllis looked perturbed. I think she was dialing Mom's number again. It wouldn't even help to have the president try dialing. Mom would be busy. Now, Dr. Phyllis looked like she was holding in an explosion. I was ushered out of her office.

When I returned home, Mom was actually present. She kissed my cheek and asked about my day. I condensed the information into an amount she could handle in her limited availability: "Fine."

"Any idea why this Phyllis person keeps calling from your school? I'm really short on time today, Danny."

"No idea, Mom. I wouldn't worry about it." I restrained a smirk.

"Good."

The conversation was already over. Before I

even finished my snack, Mom was back in her den office. I had wanted to ask her something. For some reason, I felt the need to find out about my uncle Flint, Dad's older brother. Grandma and Dad never mentioned him. Mom would be the better person to interrogate.

Vague memories of my uncle had been stirred today in class as Sara read aloud her letter to her deceased grandfather. A question had also come to mind. I texted Sara to see if she could come over. I didn't bother to check with Mom as a courtesy. She'd be on the phone and merely grunt "uh huh" to me anyway, not really hearing the question. Honestly, I could have asked my mother to invite Hitler over and she'd be like "uh huh."

Eric popped over before Sara arrived. "Clear to talk? Are you alone?"

"Don't worry. Mom's away at work at home," I assured him.

Eric understood exactly what I meant. "Great. I got Flake to get Mrs. Ellis in trouble." (Flake was our nickname for the principal, Mr. Fletcher Fisher.)

"Wow! How?"

"I claimed infringement of the medical privacy act," Eric boasted.

"English, please."

"Yeah, my dad's a lawyer. I know all about this stuff. Mrs. Ellis publicly announced that you need to consult with Dr. Phil, so I complained to Flake that Mrs. Ellis had violated your privacy and that the boys in the class were trying to defend it. I advised that she be reprimanded before my father picks up his phone to call the school. Flake turned bright red. You could feel the steam coming off the top of his head."

I high-fived Eric. "You're the man. Thanks."

Sara rang the bell. Mom popped out of the den. "Delivery?"

"No," I hollered to get her to go away.

Mom slipped back into her office. I should have told her an armed robber was at the door to see whether or not she'd do something about it. I had an even better idea. Next time, I'd say "Dad's girlfriend" and see what she'd do.

"Thanks for coming by, Sara." I ushered her in.

"Hey guys," she greeted us both.

Eric impressed Sara with his rendition of his victory over Mrs. Ellis. I politely waited for Sara's congratulations and then steered the conversation to my own agenda as we headed to the basement lounge area.

"Sara, remember the letter to your dead grandfather that you read in class today?" Sara nodded. "I also remember you once telling me a story that you communicated with him, but I don't remember the details."

"My grandpa lived with us. He was so great. He'd read to me for hours when I was small, make me laugh, play card games with me, and buy me candy and ice cream. One day he unexpectedly passed; I missed him so badly. About a month later, I snuck down to the basement with a candle. My parents were asleep upstairs. It was already midnight. I lit the candle in a holder and began chanting, 'Grandpa Brown, Grandpa Brown, Grandpa Brown' as I held a picture of him in front of me. When I stopped chanting, the room was eerily still. Not a single sound. Suddenly, the candle flickered wildly, almost dancing, and I heard my name called softly and felt a squeeze around my shoulders like a hug... Grandpa had come to me."

"A dream," commented Eric.

"It was very late at night," I added.

"I saw a flicker and heard my name," defended Sara.

"Breeze," Eric and I uttered in unison.

Sara looked hurt.

"But I do believe in that kind of stuff," I quickly interjected.

"You do?" Eric gave me an odd look.

"Once we had a barbeque in the backyard for my mother's birthday. My dad's older brother, Flint, was there. I remember my dad was grilling and Flint was sipping a beer next to my mother. I saw their shadows on the patio: My mother's was long and slender with an occasional nod of her head, but Flint's was not right. No movement of his arm holding the beer, no shadow of his head, just a dark, quivering shadow like a blob without any shape. My uncle was occasionally wiping his forehead and complaining about feeling hot."

"Was it hot?" wondered Eric.

"No one else was particularly hot or complaining."

"See," smirked Sara. "The evil shadow."

"Where's your uncle now?" asked Eric.

"That is what's bothering me," I answered frankly. "I never saw him again."

Eric whistled. Sara mouthed "Wow."

I continued. "It's been a sore subject. My grandmother never mentions Flint, and my dad warned me not to aggravate my grandmother under any circumstances at any time about him. And I don't know why. And if I'm lucky enough to get a word in with my mom, my own problems come first. I almost had a chance to ask her about him today. Then poof! She's back to work."

Sara pointed her finger. Mom was coming down the basement steps. I covered my mouth instinctively. To my relief, she didn't appear to have heard the conversation.

"I didn't know you had company, Danny."

"Is there a problem, Mom?"

"No, I just became aware of voices in the basement."

"Didn't you notice Eric and Sara earlier?" My tone was that of annoyance.

"Maybe. I had merely been checking for a delivery."

"So if I had let Kirk in, you wouldn't have noticed either. Good to know."

"Now Danny, don't be like that. Tonight's a busy night for me," Mom admonished.

"Isn't that something? You're busy tonight. Don't worry. I'll do my science homework independently." I faked a smile.

"That would be very helpful if you could." Mom walked back upstairs.

"She never has time to help me with science homework," I complained under my breath.

"Would she really not have noticed Kirk?" Eric was intrigued by the notion.

Kirk was a tattooed, wild-looking, fifteen-year-old that every mother wanted to keep far away from her child.

"Maybe she would have. I purposely said that to aggravate her. "Anyway, she's gone. I want to summon my own grandfather. Can you do that for me, Sara?"

Sara's eyes lit up with excitement. "Let's do it!"

Even Eric looked excited. We made arrangements to meet back at 8 p.m. after dark. This time, I informed Mom that my friends would be returning for a study group. Dad would be away at Grandma's house helping her with some repairs. I scrambled around upstairs to find a candle and took the photo of Grandma and Grandpa off the lintel, hiding the objects under my bed for later.

8 p.m. My friends promptly arrived; we hurried to the basement with notebooks under our arms as a pretense. Lights off and candle lit, we

sat down on the floor. Looking directly at Eric, Sara put a finger over her lips as a warning. I began chanting, "Grandpa Lewis, Grandpa Lewis. Grandpa Lewis, Grandpa Lewis," clutching the picture of my grandparents. Silence. Stillness. Nothing. We exchanged glances in the dim light. Eric fidgeted. Sara pushed her long bangs away from her eyes. I scratched my head.

HONK.

The three of us jumped up and looked around. The honk had sounded so close, like in my basement. Then absolute silence. Finally, I spoke. "The honk was in here. I know it was here."

"Sounded like it...That's for sure," agreed Sara.

"But we all know that's ridiculous, right?" countered Eric.

I shrugged. "I'm spooked. And it sounded like a bus honking. Not like a car horn."

We proceeded back upstairs. Mom was in the kitchen, preparing kale soup or avocado cake or something else inedible. Dad supplements the shopping and meals with food that regular people can eat. Otherwise, I would starve.

"Did you hear any honking, Mrs. Lewis?" Eric addressed Mom.

"No, I was on the phone."

I shook my head in utter disappointment.

Mom served us some soda and cookies. Long ago, she had learned to stop offering us whole wheat vegetable biscuits. My friends departed for the night, but the memory of the honking remained. The sound had been extremely close. Could it have been the dreaded gray bus?

Two nights later, we decided to summon my uncle Flint. We planned for a night Dad would not be tinkering in the basement. Once again, the candle was lit and the lights were turned off. I grasped a picture of Uncle Flint that I had found in a family album. "Uncle Flint, Uncle Flint. Uncle Flint, Uncle Flint." Not a noise. Not a sound. Eric looked ready to bail.

Sara put up her index finger. "Give it more than a minute, will you? Now shush."

Eric stopped drumming his fingers. Sara appeared to be concentrating. I looked up at the ceiling for some reason and shivered. Sara gasped. There was a flash of movement on the ceiling. Based on her reaction, Sara saw it too. Suddenly, two honks sounded. The flame of the candle went out. Eric bolted upstairs. We followed after him.

"Nothing," reported Eric from the front window.

"Well, I'm not really sure if I see the bus or not, anyway," I remarked. "But the horn did sound like a bus and extremely close by."

"I concur," said Sara.

None of us had anything more to add. We

sat around the kitchen table with some chips; soon the conversation turned to school.

Mom came out of her office and politely inquired about my friends' well-being.

"Work's over?" I was stunned.

"Have to stop working at some point," smiled Mom.

I thought your work goes on forever, I mused to myself.

CHAPTER THREE

Not before long, Mom had another work trip. When I returned home from school, Grandma would be waiting. In some respects, I was hoping to finally figure out the "bus thing," but I admit that I was becoming more and more fearful after that realistic sound of honking in the basement.

Walking home from school, I dragged my feet during the last block and opened the front door of my house ever so slowly.

"Your mother is away again as you can plainly see," Grandma snorted at the front door.

She hugged me tightly and returned to mixing cookie dough at the kitchen table. Cookies always make me happy, especially on an empty stomach after a long day at school. As Grandma used the mixer, I settled at the other end of the table and conversed with her. She actually is a pleasant person to have a conversation with (when it does not involve buses). Obviously, as a former teacher, she is also able to provide me with excellent advice for English assignments as well as proofread to spare me from losing points for all those grammar mistakes that my teacher inevitably finds. In fact, I needed Grandma's help for an English paper due in a few days.

Dinner was delicious. Everything was edible, unlike Mom's spinach and turkey burgers, eggplant casserole, and other "delicacies." Dad told a few jokes. Following dinner, I texted Eric and sat down to work on my English paper. Dad went down to the basement. Words came to me quickly; soon I had typed an entire page.

I treated myself to a game on my phone and then continued to work. The sound of honking interrupted my concentration. The honking was not from a regular car or truck: It sounded like the honking I had heard in the basement. I raced to the window. A gray bus was definitely in sight. But once again, the image was hazy and cloudy.

"Grandma!" I shouted. I stared at the bus, stopped directly in front of my house. "Grandma!" Where was she? The door of the bus did not open. I could not see clearly into the windows or identify a driver.

My heart raced. No one emerged from the bus; no one entered the bus. The bus was unlike any I had ever seen. Grandma came up behind me. I jumped. The bus was gone.

Grandma looked into my eyes, sensing I was terrified. "What is bothering you, Danny?"

I didn't want to come straight out and say that I had seen the bus. "Grandma, did you hear anything?"

Grandma pressed her lips together, looked

around, and appeared to be thinking. "Well, I heard you calling. I was finishing something in the kitchen."

"No, Grandma. Did you hear anything before I called you?"

"Yes."

Vague answer. Desperation in my voice, I continued, "Please tell me what you heard, Grandma."

"I heard you running."

I gave up. I was too tired from school to figure out if Grandma had or had not heard the honking. Returning to my room for the night, I fingered the treasured Italian alarm clock Grandpa Lewis had given me from his travels. The ticking eventually lured me to sleep.

Eric and Sara wanted to catch a glimpse of the bus too. After school, they hung around the living room, practically walking in circles. Grandma peered into the room with a funny expression on her face. The bus never made an appearance. I was not surprised. Sooner or later, I expected to be admitted to a psychiatric facility.

Frustrated that my friends had left in disappointment, I bombarded Grandma with questions. "Grandma, why am I the only one seeing goofy buses? Why doesn't Dad see them?"

"Your father is practical. He looks at what he has and not at what he does not have. He does not notice what could improve except in his inventions, of course. He never notices deficiencies in people."

Sometimes, Grandma strings words together and seems to be formulating sentences, but the content makes no sense to me, and she never clarifies the meaning. I was pretty sure, however, that Grandma was not answering my question. Furthermore, Dad is smart, all-around smart in every subject, so I didn't understand how Grandma could say that he doesn't notice things. "So how about Mom? Why can't she see the bus?"

"What about your mother!" Grandma rudely exclaimed. "Who knows what she sees or what will be? Now, let's look at that English paper of yours."

The conversation ended (once again).

By a quarter to ten, Grandma had scribbled over most of my paper. With all those revisions, I'd surely receive an A. She excused herself to retire for the night. Dad was still puttering in the basement. The doorbell rang. I peeked into the peephole and startled. A man in a dark uniform was standing on the stoop, a blue cap pulled over his eyes. His badge read "Bus Driver."

"Go away," I attempted to scream though my voice was barely audible. "Dad, Dad!" came out as a hoarse whisper.

"I'm here for a pickup," a muffled, deep-sounding voice announced through the door.

I felt frozen in place. I couldn't form words with my mouth. How I wished for Dad. A hand literally came through the door. I bolted and raced downstairs to find my father. We both returned upstairs, Dad yielding a crowbar. He flung open the front door. The stoop was empty.

Dad rubbed my back. "I'll get him if he ever tries to come back here again. I've got your back, Danny. Don't you worry about a thing." Dad remained upstairs for my reassurance.

Finally, I acknowledged the fact that I was crazy and mentally deranged but hoped I could be cured before needing to be locked up. I went to my bedroom and dialed Dr. Phyllis. Her answering service picked up.

"Is this a life-threatening situation?"

"Yes, yes, the guy almost grabbed me."

"Then you need to call the police if you are in physical danger."

"The police will not be able to see him."

"Young man, are you presently in danger?"

"I guess not."

"Are you bleeding? Are you contemplating suicide? Are you considering harming yourself? Hallucinating?"

"No...no...no...stop these questions. May I please just speak with Dr. Phyllis?"

"Not at night because you do not have a life-threatening emergency."

"Then I'll meet her at school first thing in

the morning-- if I'm still around."

"The doctor is off tomorrow. She'll be back on Thursday."

"Great. I'll be dead by then, but you don't consider that life-threatening." I threw down my phone.

"What's going on?" I had not seen Dad approach.

I was embarrassed. "Lost a bet with Eric. That's all."

CHAPTER FOUR

Dad had already left to drive Grandma back to her house. Mom would be returning any minute, having called from the taxi as she rode home from the airport. I admit I had missed her a bit. I loitered by the living room window.

A taxi pulled up to the curb. Mom emerged and grabbed a carry-on bag from the trunk. As she skipped up the steps, I flung open the front door.

"My marvelous Danny!" Mom hugged me tightly.

"I'm happy to see you, Mom. It's been a rough week."

"I'm so sorry to hear that. We will definitely need to fix that. I'm going to run to the gym for just a sec and then I'll be back before you know it."

"But I don't need you later. Later, you'll be useless. How about now?"

Mom was already grabbing her gym bag from her room. My heart felt like it had dropped a couple inches inside my chest. Before I knew it, Mom was out the door.

I stared out the window. The hazy, gray bus was right out front with the door open! "No!" I screamed. Mom probably couldn't hear me. I pounded on the window. Oblivious, Mom proceeded toward her car. Not thinking about myself, I raced out the door to protect her.

I watched in horror as the bus driver with the dark uniform and blue cap pulled over his eyes advanced toward Mom. Was she blind? She was pressing the remote of her car to open the door.

"Mom!"

The driver dragged her onto the bus before I could get to her. The door closed and the bus took off. I had been within a few feet of the bus, nearly able to touch it. I ran down the street after it, but the bus had faded, like a mist dissipating. Gone without a trace.

Immediately, I returned home and dialed Grandma. Everything made sense in retrospect. Grandma had known about the bus. That was obvious. She had been warning me, always snorting when Mom was mentioned. The only mystery was how Grandma had known about the bus when no one else had. Something else bothered me, too.

"Mom's gone," I cried frantically into the phone.

"Bound to happen," Grandma commented matter-of-factly.

"Send her back," I demanded.

"Danny, I have no control over the bus," Grandma responded most apologetically.

"Bologna. You're the only one in the world who knows about the bus."

"Danny, listen carefully. I know you're

upset. I've been through this before, but I have absolutely no control. Have your father turn around and pick me back up. He dropped me off only minutes ago. Then we can speak in person."

"Wait. Is the bus going to take me away too?" I shrieked.

"Absolutely not." Grandma's tone was confident, and I believed her.

I hung up and instantly dialed Dad. "Quick. Go back to Grandma's and bring her here."

"What's going on?" Dad was perplexed.

"Mom won't be coming home for a few more days."

"But she just called from the taxi that she was on her way."

"I know. Something about unfinished business." My lie came easy.

"Bummer. Wish I would have known before I took Grandma all the way home. Be back in a jiffy."

Grandma was right that Dad just goes with the flow. He doesn't stop to question why his wife is abruptly leaving seconds after she calls from the taxi that she's on her way home. But Dad did ask me a difficult question when he returned with Grandma. "When's Mom coming back?"

Now what could I tell him? How would I know if and when she's coming back? Maybe Grandma would know, but she would never tell. Should I have him call the bus driver? Great idea. What's his number? Instead, I was forced to continue the lie. "A few more days. She has that new back brace that's so tight that your organs start popping out of your mouth. She's probably having a hard time selling it."

"Probably right, kid. Wonder why she didn't text me."

"She asked me to tell you *in the interest of time*, her words."

"Fine." Dad was satisfied and skipped down the basement steps.

As soon as Dad was out of earshot, I asked Grandma the questions I dared not ask previously. Mom was gone, and I desperately needed answers. "How do you know about the bus? Is Uncle Flint on the bus too?"

Grandma nearly toppled over, grabbing the wall to steady herself. She stammered and stuttered. Finally, the English teacher found her words. "Yes, my son is on the bus," she conceded sadly. "And I haven't seen him since."

"Did you ever try to bring him back, like charge the bus?"

"That never occurred to me."

"How can that be?" I looked at Grandma as if she were a lunatic. Any reasonable person would have tried to get their son off the bus.

"Danny, let me start from the beginning so you can try to understand the situation. Initially, I conjured up all kinds of reasons as to why I began seeing a gray bus. Each and every day, I came up with various explanations such as shadows, mirages, mini-seizures, and dreams because no one else in the world was seeing gray buses. Then I tried to rationalize the honking. I researched ringing in the ears, ear infections, and Meniere's syndrome, but none depicted honking and definitely not honking noises with the absence of any other types of sound. A man in a dark uniform had also appeared for a pickup; I figured he might have been a real bystander.

"Then, one day, I was the scheduled speaker at an important conference at school. My car was in the shop, and I had arranged with Flint to drive me, as he was between jobs, a nice way of saying he was fired from one job and looking for another.

"As the hour got later, I dialed Flint. He didn't answer his phone. Flint was the type of person that would make an appearance at the very last minute, so I delayed calling a cab. I assumed he was out with his buddy, a Hispanic gentleman I recall. I misjudged and consequently missed the meeting. Flint parked and sauntered into the house two hours later. He said hello without even remembering that he had promised to drive me and headed to his room."

Grandma's face expressed disappointment as if Uncle Flint was letting her down at this very instant. "I told him, 'Flint, you're useless to me. Absolutely useless.' He couldn't care about anyone other than himself."

Grandma had stirred the memory of my last interaction with Mom. I had begged Mom to stay, complaining that I had had a rough week, but she ran out the door anyway.

The narrative continued. Grandma looked as if she were watching old memories flash before her eyes. "Flint emerged from his room, mumbled, and left the house."

I saw a spark of rage in Grandma's face.

"Flint left without an apology. I looked out the window. To my disbelief, the gray bus was directly out front. The driver in the dark uniform came out the bus door and walked up to Flint. Flint was distracted. I yelled for him to look, but he couldn't hear me. In an instant, Flint was dragged onto the bus and vanished into thin air."

"Exactly like Mom," I said ruefully.

"You remarked earlier that I should have charged the bus. For your information, I never saw the bus again until very recently. I always figured that even if Flint somehow managed to get off the bus, he would forget to call home. Sad, but the truth."

"Did you know the bus was coming for Mom? Why didn't you warn me?"

"I could not have known that, Danny. I considered the possibility and hoped that it was not the case, but I have no inside knowledge or ability to communicate with the bus, whatsoever. In fact, I did point out the bus to you whenever I saw it, so its existence would not take you by surprise."

I believed Grandma and understood that

she probably would not be my ticket to saving Mom.

◆ ◆ ◆

Once again, I found myself heading down to the basement with a candle. After the house was quiet for the night, I whispered, "Uncle Flint, Uncle Flint." A second time: "Uncle Flint, Uncle Flint." And a third time: "Uncle Flint, Uncle Flint." I stared intently at his photograph. He was dressed in a suit and tie for my parents' wedding. Nothing occurred. Dejected, I returned upstairs to go to bed. Something had gone wrong with the summoning process. What? Twice, the summons had worked. I thought and thought. Sara! Sara had to be involved in the process. So I would have to tell my friends that not only am I seeing an imaginary bus, but that it took both my Mom and my uncle away. The conversation should be very interesting.

I stared out my bedroom window for signs of the bus until my eyelids became too heavy to keep open.

Upon awakening, I smelled homemade pancakes. Breakfast was wonderful when Grandma was around. Dad perused the main articles in the newspaper; I scrolled the sports updates. No one mentioned Mom.

I spoke to Eric and Sara at lunch. "Got news

to tell you."

Both of them looked at me expectantly, no longer taking bites of their sandwiches.

"It's about the bus."

"Yeah..." urged Eric.

"My grandma finally admitted that she knows all about the bus."

"We figured as much," Sara commented. "Give us the new info."

"I don't even know how to say it."

"Give it to us straight," offered Eric.

"You won't believe it. You'll sing, 'He makes up stuff because he's not tough,' and call me what you call Troy..."

Just my luck, Troy, the classmate who gets under Eric's skin, happened to be walking by our table. "Say what you call me, man. Say it to my face." He glared at Eric.

"Go away, Troy," I pleaded. "We call you Troy. What do you think we call you? Gertrude? Mildred? We are talking about a different Troy. If you think you want to know what we call him, you may want to think twice."

Eric chimed in, "We not only give him a different name, we rearrange his face." Eric showed Troy a fist, and Troy took off. "Now go on with your news, Danny. That was bad timing."

"Sure was. I still don't know how to put it. Alright. Here it goes. My mom was picked up by the bus and she's gone."

"Your mom is always gone," Eric protested.

"See, that's what I was afraid you were going to say."

Sara studied my face. "For real, Danny?"

"I'm afraid so. And my uncle, too."

"Oh, come on!" Eric slapped the table. "Two relatives on an invisible bus."

"Yes. And you guys are the only ones who can help me." I felt so desperate; I think my friends could see it on my face.

"Don't worry, Danny, we'll help you," assured Sara with Eric nodding along.

On the way home from school, the wild teenager Kirk approached me. "Got fresh brownies."

I played dumb. "So you've been in the kitchen baking, huh?"

"These aren't your regular brownies." Kirk winked.

"Why? Extra chocolate?"

"Something else extra. You'll feel really, really good, man."

"What if there's too much of the extra, Kirk? What if there are other extras that you don't even know about? And do people feel good when they pass out cold after eating a brownie, Kirk?"

I surprised Kirk with my comments. He looked away stupidly. I admonished, "Watch yourself, Kirk. I don't want to one day have to step over your dead body lying in the street."

Kirk looked back at me. Something else was on his mind. "I ain't worried about dyin'. The guys who sell me the brownies know what they're doin'."

Of course they know what they are doing, I thought. The drug sellers are all chemists with a PhD who decided to go into the profession of baking brownies and carefully measure the ingredients but accidentally let a drug or two fall into the batter. Kirk was an idiot.

"I just never heard of people seein' fake things for real," Kirk began saying.

"What are you talking about?" I felt like flinging the brownies right out of his hands. Kirk seemed to already be losing his mind and expecting an eighth-grader to help him.

"I see buses pulling up to my place." Kirk wiped perspiration off his forehead with the back of his hand.

While Kirk spoke, I studied the shadows on the sidewalk. My shadow was long and slender in contrast to the indiscernible blob which should have been Kirk's shadow. I covered my mouth to stifle a gasp, alarming Kirk. "You better be careful or they'll get you. They may come to pick you up."

"Who's gonna pick me up? Do you know about that bus? It's like fuzzy. But not like fuzzy when I drink too much. A different kind of fuzziness."

"You drink too!" I nodded sadly. "Just be careful. The bus is real." What else could I tell him? He wasn't exactly going to start turning his life around.

As I turned to walk away, my mind came into sharp focus. "Kirk, do me a favor. Call me the next time you see the bus. Please. It's really important." Maybe I could get Mom back. The rest of the walk home, I imagined myself running to the bus to save Mom.

"Absolutely useless" is how Grandma had described Uncle Flint. Kirk definitely fit that description. Was Mom also useless? I didn't think so, but Grandma was able to fill all of Mom's roles when she wasn't around. I shuddered.

That night, Sara accompanied me to the basement to summon Mom. Eric was grounded at home--not that unusual of an occurrence. His dad is a lawyer, making it impossible for Eric to weasel out of anything. His parents also forbid him to go out when he gets behind on school work.

I began the process. "Mom, Mom. Mom, Mom." Absolute silence.

"She's too freshly gone. Try your uncle," suggested Sara.

"Fine."

"Uncle Flint. Uncle Flint." I studied his picture. "Uncle Flint. Uncle Flint." The suspense was overwhelming since I feared that he would not respond.

Another long minute of silence. Then a deep voice. "Well, I'm here."

I instinctively jerked away and pulled Sara with me. "The bus driver," I hissed at her, recognizing the voice.

"And so I am. Uncle Flint, as you call him, is transferring."

I saw a murky image of a dark cap and uniform in the room. "Don't touch us." I showed my clenched fists.

"You called me," the bus driver reminded in a rude tone.

"No, we didn't. We called Uncle Flint," I sneered.

"You can no longer call him by candle."

"Why not?" Sara bravely challenged.

"I already explained to you. He's transferring, and now his seat on the bus is empty."

I clenched my fists harder. "I'm warning you. We are not going to take a ride on your bus." With the dark cap pulled over his eyes, I couldn't see the expression on the bus driver's face

"I already have a pickup in mind." The bus driver's tone was jovial.

Kirk. The thought occurred to me that he might be next, but I had to focus on my own agenda. "Get my mother off your bus NOW."

"First, she needs to sit down," the bus driver

said with authority. "She needs to learn to sit down and listen."

"Why won't she sit down?" I asked in bewilderment. "Please don't hurt her; I'm begging you."

"She's exercising, or so she thinks," patiently answered the bus driver.

"Good heavens." I slapped my forehead.

Sara, the intelligent and practical one of us, interrupted. "Where is Flint transferring?"

"To the gray ship." The bus driver faded away.

"But my mother..." I protested to no avail. Now what could I do? I searched Sara's face for an answer. As she was engrossed in thought, my own thoughts returned to Kirk. "Be right back." I dashed up the stairs at top speed.

Sara yelled something after me, but I was already upstairs and could no longer hear her. I flung open the front door and raced two blocks to Kirk's house. I pounded on his door; his mother opened the door with a scowl.

"Sorry ma'am. I know it's late, but it's an emergency. Is Kirk home?"

"In name only."

I knew what she meant. Physically present, but mentally zoned out. Having a son like Kirk must be most difficult for a parent to bear.

"He's worse than usual," Kirk's mother warned. "Something is eating away at him...making him quite uneasy. I thought I had thrown it all away," she mumbled to herself sorrowfully before returning to her sarcastic, angry tone. "He never listens. He just won't listen. He's not contributing anything to this household. He's useless."

My eyes opened wide like saucers. The word "useless" echoed in my mind and terrified me. I should not have come. Too late. I turned around slowly, fearing the inevitable: The gray bus was there on the street.

I could not worry about Kirk at this moment because my priority was getting to Mom. At top speed, I reached the door of the bus, lurching forward to touch it and nearly falling over as my hand went right through the door. Frantically, I flailed my arms in every direction, unable to touch anything tangible. How I wished to bang on that door! My fists kept striking air.

"Mom, you in there? Mom?"

The door of the bus opened. Before I could raise my leg to ascend the step, I was distracted by a commotion behind me: Kirk being dragged by the man in the dark uniform and Sara running towards me, panting loudly.

"That was the very last time. I won't do drugs anymore. I promise," Kirk wailed.

"Kirk!" shrieked his mother. "Where are you going at this hour?"

I looked back at the open bus door and then again at Kirk. Who to save? What to do? I raised my leg to ascend the steps, only to be yanked and pulled away violently. Speedily, Kirk was dragged through the bus door. Less than a second later, the bus disappeared. The hands loosened from around my chest.

"Why did you pull me away, Sara? I almost got to my mother."

"You're not thinking straight, Danny. If you get on that bus, then another person will be missing. We need to get your mom back here, and we need your uncle to tell us how," Sara explained.

"My uncle is out to sea," I said bitterly.

"So what?" countered Sara. "If we can communicate with a bus, we can communicate with a ship. Just not by a candle, according to that man's rules or whatever you want to call him."

Sara never ceased to amaze me with her brains, yet I was still angry and resentful that she had prevented me from boarding the bus. "So what do we do? Go out to sea?"

"No, not exactly. I'm still thinking."

"And while you think, my mother could be transferring like my uncle Flint. They could both sink in the gray ship." Sara looked upset. I immediately apologized.

Meanwhile, Kirk's mother had been canvassing the area. "Where's Kirk? Did he get on a gray bus? Do you know what company the bus is from?"

"Didn't catch the name, ma'am."

Sara withheld a giggle. I thought Kirk's mother should go back inside and enjoy the peace.

When I returned back home, Dad was unnerved. "Mom hasn't contacted me today at all.

Something is wrong."

Grandma rubbed Dad's shoulder. "The work, Scott, you know."

"Can I help you with something, Dad?" I offered sweetly.

"May I help you?" Grandma corrected, and I groaned.

"I'm just anxious about Mom. That's all," Dad conceded.

Grandma and I exchanged knowing glances.

CHAPTER FIVE

Eric slammed his locker door. "I miss all the fun. You saw the driver, and you saw Kirk being dragged on to the bus?! I would have paid my allowance for a month to witness that."

"Yeah, it sounds way cool to you, Eric, but my mom's life is on the line."

"I'm gonna help you get her home, and from now on, no more groundings. I'll sue my own dad if I need to."

"Good luck with that. Doesn't your dad win like every case?"

"The moon!" Sara excitedly announced as she hurried over to our lockers. "The moon!"

"Not a favorite topic of mine. Sorry." For once, I thought Sara was losing it.

"No, no. That's how we are going to communicate with Flint. I stayed up late trying to figure out the solution."

"Long distance call to the moon? Doubt it will work."

"Kind of expensive trip for my budget," added Eric.

"Guys, just listen to me, will you? The crazy, dark-uniform man said we can't communicate by candle light. He also informed us that Flint was transferring to a ship. Ships are only visible at sea by the light of the moon. Tomorrow night is a full moon. We can try calling Flint by moonlight."

Sara did make sense after all. We all planned to meet at the park. I would tell Dad that I was going to Sara's house, and she would tell her father that she was coming to mine. Eric was confident he could get out of his house "one way or another," meaning he was risking getting grounded if he got caught leaving without permission.

The following night, I walked over to the park as planned. Sara was already present, dressed in a light blue sweater on this cool fall night. Eric trotted over to meet us, predictably wearing a T-shirt despite the cold, while I donned an old sweatshirt. I noted the full moon bathing us in its light.

"Ready?" Sara inquired, her arms wrapped around her chest to keep warm.

"Let's do it," Eric and I eagerly replied.

"Uncle Flint, Uncle Flint." I held a picture of my uncle as I chanted. This time I had chosen a casual picture of Flint sitting next to Grandma in case the other formal picture was not right for this summoning stuff. The picture was quite visible in the moonlight. "Uncle Flint, Uncle Flint."

Unbelievably, a gray ship appeared on the baseball field, masts and sails extending quite a distance upwards.

"Whoa!" I called out.

Sara was dumbstruck. Eric's mouth hung open.

"I'm here."

The voice startled us. We whirled around and saw nothing.

"You called?" a voice spoke indifferently.

I recognized the voice. "Uncle Flint?" I still saw nothing.

"Little man Danny."

I recalled him referring to me by that very name and not fondly.

"So what do you want? You see I'm in a bit of a predicament." The voice was coming from our right.

"Can you help me get Mom back?" I abruptly asked, disheartened by his lack of interest and uncomfortable speaking to the air. Sara was looking around intently.

"I guess we are all kind of in the same boat. Get it?" Uncle Flint laughed obnoxiously.

As Flint continued talking, I studied the distant ship. Eric was scowling; my teeth were clenched.

"I tried to warn you guys. Remember the honks? The blue guy let me warn you that your mom was going to be picked up if she didn't change her ways. And what do you know? She didn't."

"Tell me how to get my mother back." I couldn't believe this callous man was related to me.

"I have no idea whatsoever." Uncle Flint's voice was now coming from somewhere on our left. His disinterest was appalling. "Last time I saw her on the bus, she was doing her own thing and exercising. And now, I've moved on or transferred as the blue man calls it."

I held back tears, disappointed to hear twice that instead of focusing on trying to get off the bus, Mom was busy exercising.

Sara finally spoke. "Why did they transfer you, sir?" Her head tilted upwards, unsure where to address the voice.

"The rules go something like land, then sea, then air. I don't pay much attention."

"I could tell," muttered Eric. "Loser," he said under his breath.

"And then where?" Sara anxiously demanded.

"Right now I want to focus on the ship. I want to look around a bit, talk to the guys, and hang out, you know what I mean?"

"You're no help at all," Eric blasted.

The ship faded. "Uncle Flint," I called. No response. "He's worthless," I remarked to my friends. We departed for the night in absolute exasperation.

◆ ◆ ◆

The next day, Eric walked home with me

after school to work on our science project. Without Mom around to help, I would need Eric's full attention if we were going to make any progress on making our solar hot dog cooker, which involved carefully measuring and cutting a parabola and covering it with foil. While Mom is really good at assembling and measuring, I don't have the patience for it. Eric and I would have to do our best.

We had just passed the townhouse where sunflowers decorate the front lawn in the summer months; now, withered stalks were all that remained of them. I turned around at the sound of an approaching car. A BMW pulled into the driveway and a man in a fancy suit hustled out. I quickly tugged at Eric's shirt to get him to stop and look.

"Could it be the same guy who disappeared? He fits the description of a business guy," I whispered. My heart began beating faster.

"Could very well be."

Within seconds, the man entered the house and the door closed. I had every intention of charging up the stairs after him, but Eric restrained me, suggesting we think and plan before speaking with the man. Reluctantly, I agreed.

"Something is definitely wrong," Dad announced before dinner. "Mom did not answer a single call or text in four days. I'm ready to call the police."

Eric had a funny expression on his face. I

began sweating, as Eric tended to blurt out inappropriate comments; this time was no exception. "Police won't be able to get her off that bus."

I implored Eric with my eyes to stop speaking. Too late. Dad was studying both of our faces and turned to me. "Danny, do you know where your mother is? I want to know the truth."

Of course I knew where my mother was, but I also knew Dad would never accept such a reason. Lucky for Grandma, she was next door and missed being interrogated.

"Danny," Dad raised his voice. "I expect an answer."

"She's with Uncle Flint," I inadvertently let out of my mouth. Eric nodded approvingly.

"I haven't seen Flint in years. That jerk. Why would Mom be with him?"

"I don't know, Dad. I just saw Mom go on the same bus as him. I'm sorry."

"Mother!" Dad shouted as Grandma entered the house. "When did Flint come back? You didn't mention a thing to me about him."

"I haven't seen Flint in a very long time. You know that, Scott."

"I demand to know what my good-for-nothing brother is doing with my wife now." Dad was fuming like I've never seen before.

"Scott, I don't know where you got such a ridiculous notion." Grandma looked at Dad as if he were deranged.

Both Grandma and Dad faced me. My mind

raced. I took a risk. "The businessman who lives down the block in the townhouse with sunflowers in the summertime came home from the bus. (Grandma gasped and thankfully Dad did not notice.) He told me he saw Mom on the bus, but I guess Mom and Flint must still be traveling."

"I don't know any businessman down the block!" Dad roared. "And don't tell me that your mother is taking tours on a bus with Flint."

"I hardly know this man either," I admitted. (In actuality, I don't know him at all.) "But we should make an effort to go over to speak with him because, honestly, I have no idea what Mom or Flint are doing on the bus, and that is the truth, Dad."

Eric nodded in agreement.

"Fine." Dad grabbed a light jacket. "Let's go."

Eric jabbed me with his elbow as we left the house. "Smart thinking."

Maybe we would get answers. Dad knocked on the door of the townhouse.

"Wait. Let me speak first," I suggested as we eagerly awaited a response.

Thank goodness, the businessman himself opened the door and not the crabby, old lady. His demeanor was casual, but his eyes belied that he did not recognize us. "What can I do for you folks?"

The old lady approached. I recoiled and closed my eyes in dread. "Who's at the door, sweetheart?"

Sweetheart? I reopened my eyes to find the old woman's knobby fingers gently stroking the man's back. Surely, she must have schizophrenia. One minute mean and crazy, the next minute nice and tame.

The man turned toward her. "I'm trying to figure out who they are, Mother."

I spoke quickly, showing a wallet-sized picture of Mom. "I thought you may recognize my mother. We live down the block and haven't heard from her in days. Is it possible you may have seen her on a bus?" I winked at him.

"Yes, I've seen her jogging down the block... sometimes even in the pouring rain...Not too many other people do that."

That's my crazy Mom. I was embarrassed.

Eric interjected. "Have you seen her on that bus...you know?" He also winked. "You'd remember a lady exercising instead of sitting down, right?"

Dad erupted again. "How would you know if my wife was sitting, standing or climbing the walls?"

Eric stuttered. The man was uncomfortable.

"Listen, gentlemen," interrupted the businessman. "You are standing on my porch stoop, so I want to know exactly what you want from me."

Dad returned his attention to the man. "Sorry, sir. The boys thought you may have information on my wife's bus ride."

"I drive to work. I don't take the bus."

The BMW was still parked in the driveway. I admired it from the stoop.

"Jim," piped his mother. "Maybe they are referring to when you were traveling all that time... when I gave up on you...That's what I think they are talking about."

"I apologize, but I cannot remember those travels clearly. The doctor suggested some amnesia." The man shrugged but had a faraway look, as if a memory did surface.

"Bummer." I was disappointed. The businessman had been our best hope because he had succeeded in getting off the bus and could shed light on how Mom might be able to do the same.

Dad's eyes teared a bit. "Thank you, sir. Have a good evening. Let's go boys."

Despite our protests, Dad decided to call the police. "Danny, I don't understand. Don't you want your mom back?"

"Sure I do, Dad, but the police may not be able to reach her."

"Let the police make that determination," Dad argued.

Grandma, Eric, and I watched as Dad picked up his phone to call the police station, and then we slipped into the kitchen. I informed Grandma that Uncle Flint was transferred to a gray ship. She listened in fascination.

"After Flint disappeared, I never heard from him again. How is he?" Grandma eagerly inquired.

"Not very helpful, I'm sorry to say."

Grandma nodded sadly. "Probably why they transferred him."

CHAPTER SIX

Per my request, Sara unsuccessfully re-attempted to summon Mom in the basement. "Why won't she answer?" I was so frustrated.

"Wish I could help, man," Eric said sincerely. "Too bad your uncle can't trouble himself to help you with his own sister-in-law."

"Danny, maybe your grandmother could try to summon your mother. She seems to have more experience with this bus thing than we do," Sara considered.

"Not sure. That idea never crossed my mind before. We can try her."

We ran back upstairs to find Grandma. She was reading some old English book in the living room. "Why do you read that stuff if you are no longer in school? You should pick out a fun book."

Grandma patted the book cover. "This is a most excellent piece of literature. A work of art. The descriptions are colorful, vivid."

"I bet," commented Eric.

"Anyway, Grandma, we need your help. Could you please try to contact Mom?"

Grandma looked uncertainly at Sara and Eric.

"Don't worry. They're both completely in on this bus thing, Grandma. Can you help us?"

"Danny, I've never been able to communicate with Flint like you have. I was merely able to see other people boarding the bus. How would I call Flint or your mother? Stand in the kitchen and shout, 'Oh Flint? Oh Sherry?' Send them a letter addressed to the bus? Flint didn't even bother to answer me while he was still at home!"

"How about calling him at night, in the dark, Mrs. Lewis?" Eric hinted.

"On my phone? What difference would the dark make?"

I apologized to Grandma for bothering her. She obviously didn't know how to summon people like Sara did. We had left the summons part out when discussing Flint with her. I think Grandma assumed that we had seen a gray ship on the street or something like that.

I ushered my friends back to the basement. We had all believed that Grandma would have been able to contact Mom when the truth was that she had not a clue.

"Kirk!" I suddenly shouted. "And if that doesn't work, I'm boarding the bus."

My friends looked at me like I was delusional for suggesting boarding the bus, but they helped me obtain a photo of Kirk from his mother by concocting a story about showing his picture around the neighborhood.

Once again, we hurried down the basement

steps and sat on the floor. I concentrated on Kirk's photo, and Eric held the candle. Sara chanted, "Kirk Meadow, Kirk Meadow. Kirk Meadow, Kirk Meadow."

The silence was nerve-racking.

"Kirk Meadow, Kirk Meadow..."

"I'm here," laughed a voice.

"Him again! Move back guys," I ordered, standing up bravely. I took the candle from Eric to reveal the bus driver with the dark uniform. "We called Kirk Meadow, not you. Let us speak with him now." I was enraged.

"He's transferring," answered the bus driver.

"How convenient," Eric mumbled

"I don't think he is," I argued.

"Oh, he is. And if he doesn't listen real soon, he'll be on the gray rocket to..."

"Keep going whack job. A gray rocket to where?" Eric came to stand by my side, his fist raised to fight if needed.

"To oblivion and beyond," the bus driver cackled and faded away.

While Eric mocked the driver's absurd dialogue, I felt anguished by his disappearance. "Get him back, Sara. I'm going to demand to board the bus."

"No you're not, Danny. Let's think things through very carefully," Sara said firmly.

"OK. We'll wait thirty days to speak with Kirk on the ship by the light of the next full moon. What do I tell my dad in the meantime? That's not going to work," I retorted angrily.

"Kirk's messed up, Danny. I wouldn't count on him. Listen to Sara," Eric advised.

I stomped and fumed. "Call him back, Sara. Now."

Sara looked frightened by me. I had overstepped. "So sorry, Sara. Really sorry."

"I need to go." Sara quickly skipped upstairs. I heard the front door close.

"Get a grip, Danny," Eric warned me. "You'll mess everything up, and Sara won't want to help you anymore."

I begrudgingly admitted that Eric was right. I had made things worse. Worse yet, when I headed upstairs, two officers were speaking with Dad about Mom's disappearance. "Oh no," I uttered.

A stocky cop, Officer Moore, looked at me curiously. "Oh no," he repeated sarcastically. "Aren't you happy I'm here to help you find your mother?"

"Of course I am." I couldn't think of anything else to say.

"Your father's brother disappeared years back and now his wife. Coincidental? I think not."

Dad was becoming furious. "What are you suggesting? That I eliminate family members?!"

"We need to cover all our bases," elaborated the taller, thinner officer named Officer Miller.

"No phone calls whatsoever. No purchases on credit cards. No activity on the internet," added Officer Moore.

Dad turned pale. "She's dead?"

"No, she's not dead, Dad," I assured him. Eric nodded.

Officer Moore eyed me. "Anything you want to tell us, young son?"

"I mean that my mother is always going somewhere. She travels a lot for business, and even when she's home, she's not really home because she leaves to go to the gym or someplace else, and she doesn't even answer her phone like when my teachers call...so just because she is not home, doesn't mean she's dead."

"That may be one possibility," Officer Miller conceded, "although we can't find any travel records or gym sightings recently. But we have a second angle." The officer looked at Dad. "Do you know anything about George, Stuart, Jim, Trent or Ron?"

Dad's formerly-pale face turned scarlet. "Now what are you insinuating?"

"We do not insinuate, aggravate, irritate, berate..."

"Get to your point," Dad demanded.

"We collect evidence. These are some of your wife's contacts."

"One's her ex. Another may be a trainer at the gym. She's married to me, you know." The volume of Dad's voice steadily increased.

"How about Trent?" interrogated Officer Moore. "He's out of town."

"You're wasting your time," I insisted to the officers."

"Is that so?" challenged the stocky Officer Moore.

Eric came to my assistance. "Hey, Danny just finished explaining this to you, but you're not getting it. Let me try. I know Mrs. Lewis. I'm at Danny's house all the time, and she's never around, like almost never. Always working or doing something, so this is like normal for her."

"Do you wish to add anything else?" Officer Moore was studying Eric's face. He fidgeted.

"Actually, yeah. We think Danny's mother is with Flint. If you can find Flint, you'll have no trouble finding Mrs. Lewis. Can you swim?" Eric laughed; I stifled a giggle.

The officers were not the least bit amused. Dad wasn't either.

"Swim? Did you throw a body into the lake?" Officer Miller asked seriously.

"Of course he didn't," Dad snapped. "Enough. I called you officers over to assist me. My son and his friend are not involved in my wife's disappearance. This ridiculous questioning is only serving to make me more upset."

The officers were ushered out of the house. Dad implored Eric to return home.

Dad confided in me, "All I wanted them to do was find your mother. Now I don't know if I'm more sad or furious."

I hugged Dad firmly. "I'll help you find

Mom."

❖ ❖ ❖

I borrowed money from Dad to purchase a box of Sara's favorite chocolates on my way home from school. She had been ignoring me at school. I walked over to her house and knocked on the front door.

"Sara is not receiving guests today," her mother relayed to me.

"I know I upset Sara, and I'm so, so sorry. I didn't mean to at all. I just came by to drop off a gift as an apology if she would please accept it."

"That's most kind, Danny. I'll be sure to give it to her."

"Thank you, and make sure she reads the note."

My attached note was brief and to the point. "Sorry I was a jerk. I am going to attend jerk, buffoon, and know-it-all rehab every day."

Within fifteen minutes, Sara called to thank me. Losing her friendship (and brains) was almost worse than losing my mother.

CHAPTER SEVEN

Life changed into a new routine. Grandma replaced Mom, washing my clothes, advising me on school issues, and preparing my meals. I still thought about Mom but not as often. Dad tinkered around happily in the basement. I didn't particularly notice him to be withdrawn, sad, or dragging his feet. At night, I occasionally listened by the window for honking noises but never heard any.

The next full moon, however, stirred me into action. I texted Sara and Eric. "Meet me at the park. Quick."

"Don't get your hopes up," Eric cautioned me at the park. We summoned Kirk by moonlight. "Kirk Meadow, Kirk Meadow. Kirk Meadow, Kirk Meadow."

I yielded a bat just in case the bus driver would appear and decide to get too close for comfort.

"Kirk Meadow, Kirk Meadow. Kirk Meadow, Kirk Meadow."

The frightful silence. One long minute. Two more minutes.

The man in the dark uniform appeared

again.

"Stay back!" I ordered.

"No, you must come close to see this," the bus driver declared.

I grunted. Sara asserted, "We will stay where we are."

"Suit yourself. Kirk has just completed the entire transfer process. Now, for the grand send-off," announced the bus driver.

"Kirk was transferring to a ship the last time we saw you. What exactly are you talking about now?" Sara was becoming agitated.

The bus driver ignored Sara. "Good-bye, Mr. Meadow. So long. Farewell. Adios. To oblivion and beyond."

"You're messed up, man," Eric derided.

We heard a powerful, explosive-like sound like a rocket growing progressively fainter.

"To oblivion and beyond," the bus driver cheered and clapped his hands.

"A real psycho," I told Eric.

Something clinked as it hit the ground. We all looked down at the source of the noise: a key attached to a blue plastic tag. As we looked back up, the bus driver was gone.

Eric fingered the key lightly, cautiously, in case it was electrified or hot. Determining it was not, he picked it off the ground. "What's this about?"

I shrugged. We looked at Sara, who was con-templating.

"Something to do with Kirk," she mused. "Do you guys think Kirk is gone for good?"

"So says the maniac," I responded

We collectively decided that it was not too late to knock on Mrs. Meadow's door.

"Did this key happen to belong to your son?" Eric politely asked, displaying it in his hand.

Mrs. Meadow immediately recognized the key. "Yes, how'd you get it? Have you found Kirk?"

Eric and I looked at each other. We had not planned for difficult questions, merely seeking confirmation that the key had belonged to Kirk.

Sara took charge. "An old friend of Kirk's saw us and knew we lived nearby. He claimed Kirk left it somewhere. He apologizes for holding on to the key for so long."

Mrs. Meadow's eyes teared up. "The key is to his grandmother's house. He used to stop by a few times a week and help her out for a couple hours until the day she was hospitalized. That was the very same day Kirk disappeared."

"Sorry, so sorry." What else could we say?

"Hold on to the key until Kirk comes home," Sara said encouragingly while rubbing Mrs. Meadow's shoulder. The distressed mother smiled faintly.

Once out of earshot of the Meadow home, Sara made sense of the confusion. "I think that key was literally the key to keeping Kirk around."

"Go on," I urged, unsure of her point.

"Listen. As soon as Kirk's grandmother is

hospitalized, poof...the bus comes to pick him up and he disappears from the face of the earth."

"Meaning..." Eric probed.

"Meaning that the fact that Kirk used to help his grandmother kept him around. As soon as his grandmother goes to the hospital, Kirk becomes useless to society, and the bus picks him up. This all makes perfect sense. Kirk was a druggie, a good-for-nothing, you know."

"So the bus driver sends him to oblivion but can't keep the key because the key is associated with something good. I get it." Eric smiled.

"I believe so," confirmed Sara.

"He's never coming back," I surmised. The thought was terrifying. "Help me summon my uncle again, Sara. I don't want my mother sent to oblivion and beyond, wherever that is."

Sara agreed and we returned to the park. The moon was now hidden by the clouds, the dark of the night intensifying.

"Uncle Flint, Uncle Flint. Uncle Flint, Uncle Flint."

The man in the dark uniform returned.

"Oh no," I groaned, too angry to be scared. "I called my uncle, not you. Your name is not Flint. Why don't you do your own thing and leave us alone?"

"This is not a telephone company," retorted the bus driver. "You don't get to keep calling people."

"Well, you're not a bus company either.

Normal bus companies don't go around picking up innocent people and never letting them off," chastised Eric.

Sara also became emboldened. "Send Danny's mother back. She doesn't belong with druggies and losers."

"I'm the driver. You don't get to give me orders."

"Where's your bus?" I challenged.

"Yeah, let's see if you really have Danny's mom," Eric taunted.

"I have her alright," insisted the driver. "She's not rehabilitated yet and may never be. Maybe I'll transfer her soon..."

"NO. Don't you dare. Show me the bus now." I was infuriated.

A flash. The gray bus appeared on the grass, about thirty feet away. Faces in the windows were visible; features were not. A slim figure was darting back and forth in the aisle. "Mom!" I cautiously began walking toward the bus. Somehow, the driver, who only moments before was standing before us, now blocked the door of the bus.

I didn't care. The bus game had gone on for too long. I began running toward the bus.

"Stop," Sara shrieked. "Stop."

"Don't do it, Danny," Eric shouted. "Don't be crazy."

Ignoring the protests of my friends, I charged at the door, not making bodily contact with the driver, ascending the first step and then the next, my eyes adjusting to the interior of the bus, lit up in contrast to the dark outside. Amazingly, I sighted my mother. She was doing jumping jacks in the aisle. *Crazy woman* was my initial thought, but I needed to focus. "Quick, Mom, run off the bus."

Probably delighted to run, Mom obeyed without hesitation. A dog bounded after her. The driver was nowhere in sight. I didn't know dogs were allowed to ride buses. Next, I watched as an unkempt man, a boy my age, and a guy in his forties also exited the bus, all squeezing by me.

"Wait for me!" I yelled. My mother was sprinting away outside. I sped down the bus steps; the door was now closed. I pushed hard. The door did not budge. I pushed even harder. The door did not even rattle or shake. Darn. I quickly found the door lever. It wouldn't move an inch. I looked around. This was clearly not an ordinary bus although the steering wheel seemed typical. Curious buttons comprised the dashboard, some labeled, others not. A small, computer-like screen sat atop the dashboard. Rows of numbers from one to sixty-six were located to the left of the driver's seat beneath the window region, presumably corresponding to the seat numbers.

I peered around the bus. The windows were now darkened; I could no longer see any people or scenery through them. A feeling of terror overtook me. "Help me. Somebody help me," I screeched. Frantically, I pressed 911 on my cell phone. The phone was dead.

I was startled by a figure walking toward me even though the man himself did not appear threatening in the least. He had a serious look about him, clean-shaven with oversized, black-rimmed glasses. A tuft of his brown, curly hair was out of place.

"I have the most interesting reading material for your bus ride if you would like," the man genially offered.

"Actually, I would like to get OFF this bus," I clarified.

"Look at this magazine." The man excitedly waved a copy of *Birdwatching* in front of my eyes. "It includes a comprehensive list of birds that live in this region. For example, did you know that the yellow-bellied flycatchers live in the woods not too far from here?"

"Sir, do you know you are on a bus for losers?"

"Let me tell you something else. The smallest bird in the world is the bee hummingbird. It's only two inches long."

"Do you work or do anything useful with your life?"

"Mourning warblers pretend to have broken wings as a distraction to their predators."

The man had given me my answer. He was useless to society. I had told him that I needed to get off the bus, and all he could do was talk about birds. I let him keep talking and amusing himself. He didn't even notice me pass to investigate the other passengers. I found a middle-aged, obese man with two chins napping in the seventh row.

In the ninth row, two women were gossiping. "Can either of you help me get off this bus, please?" I begged.

"You look like a Lewis!" the heavier woman exclaimed. "I went to school with Flint Lewis. You wouldn't believe the shenanigans and all the trouble that he made."

"Can you please help me get off this bus?" I repeated.

"Flint went out with Ann, remember Trudy?" the other woman commented.

These people were unbelievably messed-up. In the last row, I noticed a teenage boy on his phone. "Hey," I greeted, hoping to be able to communicate with someone closer to my age.

"Yeah, man." The teenager did not even look up, his face staring at his phone screen as if in a trance.

"Any way we can get off this bus, man? I'm sure you have class tomorrow," I tried to reason with him.

The teenager started laughing to himself, absorbed in some video clip. "Sick, like really cool." He repeatedly swiped and tapped the screen. "I knew they'd lose. The stupid manager changed the batting order."

"You can't possibly be on your phone twenty-four hours a day," I admonished.

Snickering. Chuckling. Swiping. Tapping. Giggling. Gasping. No eye contact. No communication with me.

I plopped into an empty seat and cried. I wasn't ashamed of my tears because no one would even notice.

PART II

CHAPTER EIGHT

"Honey, I'm home," Sherry called down the basement stairs.

Scott Lewis ascended the steps. "Oh my goodness, where were you?" He stared at his wife in disbelief. They both headed to the living room, but neither sat down.

"You know, business."

"Business! It's been weeks. You didn't call or text even once."

"I didn't?"

"No, you didn't." Scott was quite upset, hands on hips. "You should know I have the police involved."

Sherry looked confused. "There's no reason to call the police if I go away on business."

"Going away on business is not the problem, but if you forget to come back, I will certainly call the police." Scott was distracted by some background noise. "What's going on up here?"

"Nothing I know about."

A small Lhasa apso ran by. "You got a dog! You suddenly get a conscience and decide to come home, and then you buy a dog without consulting me. Sherry, what's wrong with you?"

"Honestly, I don't know anything about the dog. I need to exercise. I think I was on my way to the gym."

"THAT'S ENOUGH," Scott yelled. "ENOUGH. You and I need to talk. You cannot disappear, suddenly reappear, and then go off to exercise."

"Business, Scott. That's all. Please try to not be so angry."

The dog ran back into the room, knocking the base of a floor lamp and causing it to nearly topple over.

"Get the dog to sit. Sit, you stupid dog," Scott commanded as the dog ran out of the room. "Wait, I hear something else."

Scott rushed toward the kitchen. "What are you doing in my house?" he bellowed at a man in his forties.

"Fixing a snack, that's all," cordially replied the man.

"THIS IS MY HOUSE."

"I'm not trying to take your house away from you." The man opened a cabinet and pulled out a bag of chips.

Scott grabbed the chips away. "I would like those for work tomorrow, if you don't mind."

"Sure." The man handed them back and scrounged around until he found a box of crackers. "Guess this will have to do."

Scott was fuming. He called Sherry into the kitchen. "Who is this man?"

"Trent."

"Trent," shrieked Scott, recalling the mention of an unknown Trent by the police.

"I don't know him that well," Sherry explained. "He was on my bus and sometimes I would see him at the gym."

"Then why is he in my house?" Scott hollered.

"Lower your voice, Scott. Danny will be terrified of your yelling."

"Danny. Now that you mention him, he was out with his friends, and I didn't hear him come home. He always says hello when he returns, but I noticed his bedroom door was closed...One minute." Scott marched down the hall and flung open Danny's bedroom door. "SHERRY, GET OVER HERE."

Sherry nonchalantly entered the room.

"THIS IS NOT MY DANNY!"

A boy, also about thirteen years old, lounged on Danny's bed, wearing large headphones.

"Sherry, I'm going to the basement and when I return upstairs, I expect all these guests of yours to be out of my house, and then we are going to have a very long conversation."

Scott texted Danny and walked down to the basement to clear his mind and try to figure things out. He sat at his workbench. His foot unexpectedly hit something. Bending over to investigate, he found an unkempt, homeless-looking man curled up under the table.

"SHERRY," Scott again yelled, racing up the steps. He found Trent reading a newspaper at the kitchen table. The dog was scratching at the couch. "SHERRY!" Scott noticed a small note placed by the decorative table at the front entry hall: "Went to the gym; be back soon. Love, Sherry".

Seething, Scott returned to check Danny's room. The strange kid was still relaxing on Danny's bed. "Can you get me a soda?" the kid requested.

Can I get him a soda? Sure, I can give him an allowance too, Scott mumbled angrily under his breath. *Maybe I'll pay for his college while I'm at it. I don't even know his name.*

Again, Scott tried to contact Danny through his cell phone, becoming increasingly worried as the hour got later. No answer. Scott had been hopeful that Danny would somehow be able to shed some light on all of this insanity.

Fifteen more minutes would be the max and then Scott would have no other option other than to do the unthinkable to a teenage boy: call his friends to check up on him. Meanwhile, he would kick out all of these people and animals, starting with Trent.

Trent was still in the kitchen reading the newspaper, calmly sipping coffee out of Scott's favorite mug. The dog was licking crumbs beneath the table. "GET OUT," Scott roared.

Trent looked up stupidly from the newspaper. "I'm honestly quite comfortable just where I am." He then continued to skim another article.

Unbelievable, thought Scott. He dialed Sherry's cell phone, which immediately went to voicemail. He kicked a chair in rage. Sherry never did answer her phone while exercising despite an incident a few years back when Scott had rushed Danny to the hospital after falling down the stairs and had failed to reach her.

Maybe Scott could manage the simplest problem. "Animal control," Scott requested on the city hotline. "Yes, I need a strange dog to be picked up at once from my home...In two to three days? No way. What if I had a dangerous bear in my home? You'd let the bear roam around for two to three days and attack whomever it wanted including small, innocent children...No, I'm not being unreasonable...OK, this is totally reasonable. I'll bring the dog to you. Just give me the address." The phone call was terminated. "Dang it."

"No you don't," Scott threatened, seeing the dog raise a back leg. Too late. A puddle formed on the kitchen floor. "Bad dog. Terrible dog." The dog ran down to the basement. "Wait, don't touch my stuff down there."

Mentally drained and physically exhausted, Scott chased the dog down the steps. The unkempt man was fiddling around at Scott's work table. Scott pointed his index finger at him. "You are leaving this very instant, and there will be no discussion whatsoever. Do you hear me?"

"Not so well, I'm deaf in the left ear and partially deaf in the right one."

"Then read my lips. OUT." Scott also displayed his fists.

"I lost my cane," protested the homeless man.

"Well, you're making me lose my mind, so we're even," sneered Scott. "GET OUT NOW."

"No coat either."

The dog was now asleep under Scott's workbench. The homeless man's eyes were beginning to close as well. There would be no way to drag either of them up the steps. Scott marched back upstairs in disgust.

"Done eating MY food yet?" Scott ridiculed Trent.

"Yeah, I'm good." Trent replied good-naturedly and patted his stomach.

Scott's cell phone beeped with a text from Sherry: "Found new kick-boxing class, be back a tiny bit later than usual." Again, Scott's return call went to voicemail. He was angrier than ever before.

By now, Trent had settled into the recliner in front of the television, legs elevated.

"Beyond belief," Scott muttered to himself.

Returning to Danny's room, Scott prayed the teenager had been an apparition. Instead he received an order immediately upon opening the door: "Still waiting on the soda, dude." Scott yanked off the kid's headphones.

"Time to go home, buddy."

The kid stared blankly.

"THIS IS NOT YOUR HOUSE. DO I LOOK LIKE YOUR DAD?"

"I'm better off on my own," declared the teenager.

"HOW IS INVADING MY HOUSE BEING ON YOUR OWN?"

"All I asked for was a soda, man. You don't have to go off the deep end."

"That is it. That is it." Scott left the room in a huff and called Eric's home. Eric's mother gave him Eric's cell number, which he promptly dialed. "So sorry to bother you. This is Danny's father. Have you seen him? It's really important that I speak with him."

Eric was over at Sara's house and had been discussing the possibility that Danny's father might call looking for him. Eric muted the call. "He's on the phone. What do I say to him?"

"We were in the middle of trying to figure that out," Sara replied quietly.

Scott impatiently yelled into the phone. "Come on, Eric. What's going on?"

"Quick, Sara. The bus trip option or the other?"

"The other," Sara chose.

"The other," Eric said into the phone.

"What? Where is Danny?" Scott demanded.

"Danny went somewhere else. He's not

here...I mean I'm at Sara's. Do you want to try calling one of his other friends?" Eric suggested.

"Tell me where he is or I'm coming over," threatened Scott.

"One second." Eric muted the phone as Scott raged. "He's gonna come over," Eric frantically warned Sara.

Sara grabbed the phone. "Mr. Lewis, this is Sara. All we can do for you is tell you exactly what we saw. We are so sorry. You should know that we were trying to figure out how to help you even before you called."

"Just tell me where Danny is so I can bring him home. No more funny business."

Sara paused to consider. "I'm just going to tell him the truth," she whispered to Eric.

"Tell me right now," Scott shouted.

Sara similarly recalled Danny losing his temper with her. "OK, OK. Please keep in mind that this is exactly what we saw." She paused.

"TELL ME NOW!"

"Fine." Sara was forced to continue. "Danny boarded a bus. We saw some people getting off, including someone who looked like your wife. We yelled and screamed for him not to board, but Danny wouldn't listen."

"What bus number?"

Sara looked pleadingly at Eric and stammered. "The bus stopped at Eagle Park."

"The 39?" Scott was hopeful that he would get some detailed information. "The bus that runs a block east of the park?"

"No, not that one. A gray bus at the park."

Eric closed his lips together tightly, unsure how the conversation would progress.

"I'm unaware of a bus that stops directly in front of the park."

"That makes two of us," Eric commented, and Sara shushed him.

"To repeat, Mr. Lewis, this bus did stop at the park. It was unnumbered. You should ask your wife about it because we saw her get off it." Sara mouthed "Help" at Eric, who took the phone back.

"Eric again. Mr. Lewis, we have a great big test tomorrow. Like the hardest one of the year. If we hear anything about Danny, we will call you immediately. Have a good night." He abruptly ended the call.

Quickly, Scott searched the internet for all the bus lines passing near the park. Only the 39 did as he had surmised. He telephoned the transit authority. "Can you please tell me which bus number stops at Eagle Park?"

He was informed that the 39 was his best bet, taking him within a block of the park. "But my son boarded a bus at the park itself."

"We don't manage school buses or other private companies, sir."

"No, it was a public bus. A gray one."

"Not ours, sir."

"Then whose?"

"I recommend that you ask that question of your son when he gets home."

"THAT'S THE ISSUE. HE DIDN'T COME HOME."

"Well, I wouldn't come home either if my father had your lungs. I bid you a good night."

"Wait!" Scott was so frustrated.

A key sounded in the lock; Sherry had returned home. The dog was asleep on the living room sofa. "Useless critter," Scott scolded. Trent was snoring in the recliner in front of the television. Scott kicked his leg.

"Can't a guy get a snooze?" whined Trent.

Sherry cheerily entered the living room and attempted to hug Scott. "Missed you." He backed away.

"Sherry," Scott began in an even tone, exerting much effort to control his voice from erupting in a sonic boom. "While you were exercising, I could not find a quiet corner ANYWHERE (one boom escaped) in my own house."

"So sorry to hear that," Sherry responded in her well-trained, business-like tone reserved for disgruntled customers. "I'll..."

"No, Sherry. I'm giving the orders now," Scott interrupted. "First, I want the number of every bus you were on starting with today. Second, I want every last person and animal out of this house within the next thirty minutes. Third, you will not exercise at the gym, jog around the town, or move a single muscle unless you are able

95

to be contacted, meaning you better answer your phone if you know what's good for you. And don't you dare leave in the middle of any discussion with me ever again, and, finally, if you want to retain custody of your son, you will need to know EXACTLY WHERE HE IS." At the mention of his son, Scott lost all composure.

Sherry was speechless, a combination of feeling shocked by the demands and insulted by her husband's ranting. "I have no answer for you, Scott," she finally responded. "I can't tell you what bus I was on because the memory is hazy."

"Why does your exercise always take precedence over our family?" Scott blasted.

"I didn't realize my exercise was harmful to the family..."

"AND NOW YOUR SON IS MISSING."

"No," Sherry wailed, "that can't be true."

The discussion was useless and a waste of precious time. Scott walked away from his crying spouse in revulsion and called the police. Officers Moore and Miller made an appearance.

"Can't keep track of your family?" Officer Moore teased.

Scott restrained a punch as he ushered the officers into the dining room. Sherry sat at the table, head in her hands.

"Nice dog," commented Officer Miller, admiring the Lhasa apso, which was visible in the kitchen. Scott growled.

"No one else is missing from a bus," Officer

Moore countered to Scott's complaint of a missing son on a runaway bus. "Furthermore, no bus runs at the supposed site of the disappearance. And to top it off, your wife can't seem to recall the number of the bus she was riding or where she went!"

"We can arrest you for scamming officers of the law," threatened Officer Miller.

"Wait. Let's question the spouse a bit more. Mrs. Lewis, can you recall one stop, a single stop at any point on your bus ride?"

Sherry picked up her head. "The bus was not the stopping kind."

"Oh, how interesting, a bus that doesn't let people off. Let's arrest the bus," giggled Officer Moore. "We have one more end to tie up. Miller, call that guy in here. If he can't help, I'm considering your suggestion of making an arrest on grounds of wasting police time."

"The sleeping guy? Sure." Officer Miller walked into the living room and tapped Trent's shoulder. Trent groaned and returned to sleep. Officer Miller proceeded to shake him.

"Can't a guy get some rest?" Trent complained.

"You're going to get plenty of rest in a jail cell if you don't cooperate," hissed Officer Miller.

"Alright, what do you want?"

"Tell us about the bus you were on." Officer Moore joined Officer Miller at Trent's side. Trent looked up stupidly.

"I don't really remember."

Officer Moore slapped Trent's face. "Remember now?"

Trent looked down. The dog entered the room. "Should we question him?" Officer Moore asked sarcastically, pointing at the dog.

"He was on the bus too," Trent admitted frankly.

"Was he full or half fare?" quipped Officer Miller. "This is ridiculous."

"They were all drugged," Scott surmised, entering the living room. "Nothing else makes any sense."

Just then, the thirteen-year-old boy passed by in the hallway holding a can of soda, his headphones, set to the highest volume, emitting a sound audible to all the others.

"Hey, come over here," Officer Miller ordered.

The boy continued walking, unable to hear. Officer Miller jogged toward him and grabbed his arm. The boy jumped. His headphones were thrust off.

"This is my house. What do you want?" the boy sneered.

"Remember, this is my house," Scott corrected.

"Whatever," mumbled the boy.

Officer Moore waddled over. "What does he have to say?"

"Nothing useful yet," grumbled Officer Miller.

"Were you on this bus, and if so, can you tell me why?" demanded the stocky cop.

"Something like my dad's a drunken fool and my mom's a party girl, so I make my own decisions. Got that, officer?" The boy stared directly into Officer Moore's eyes.

"Got it. Just tell us which bus you were on." Officer Moore stared back with almost pleading eyes.

"I was listening to music. I don't remember."

"Which bus did you board?" Officer Moore was exasperated.

The boy merely shrugged.

"I've got a homeless man in my basement..." Scott began to suggest to the police.

"Bet you do. Likely drunk as a skunk. Got anyone with at least half a brain around here that can give us some useful information?" scoffed Officer Miller.

Officer Moore interrupted. "Listen, man. I do believe your son has gone missing. I see it on your face, but it might have something to do with your company."

"My company! These people were most certainly not invited to my house."

Officer Moore made eye contact with Officer Miller, who nodded to express his agreement. "Try cleaning up house if you know what I mean, and your son might be a bit more comfortable at the idea of returning home."

Scott opened his mouth to object when Officer Miller assured him, "We will undoubtedly keep searching for your son. However, we do not suspect foul play. No indications at all. As Moore said, the kid just probably got a bit uncomfortable around here with your *company*."

"Makes perfect sense," Officer Moore reiterated, waving his finger at Trent and the teenager.

As Scott fumed, trying to formulate an argument, the police officers took their leave, and he was left with the "company." "Sherry," he yelled. No answer. Scott found his wife fast asleep on the bed. The dog leaped onto his side of the bed and made itself comfortable. Scott snarled at it.

CHAPTER NINE
(ON THE BUS)

I calmed down, all of my tears used up. The bus had glass windows, but all I could see through them was something like fog or clouds. Was the bus moving? I couldn't be sure. The bus's occupants were still engrossed in their useless activities.

"Game boy," I called to the teenager. No answer. "Or maybe your name is movie man." No response. I couldn't see his phone screen, but I doubted it displayed anything important.

"Hey dude, did you see the rat run by your foot?" Still nothing. He probably wouldn't hear a smoke detector or carbon monoxide alarm either. He'd burn alive in a fire. That wouldn't be much of a loss of life.

Oh no. The birdman was approaching me. "Listen to this. It's a painted bunting's call." He played it on his phone, grinning in delight.

"Don't you realize you are a prisoner on this bus?" I snapped.

"Listen to the next bird call. Try to guess the bird. I guessed it correctly on my first try."

Sure enough, his phone played the call of a

different bird. "Why don't you try calling the police, weirdo? Are you gonna sit on this bus looking at birds forever?"

"Recognize this?" The birdman pulled a bird feather out of his pants' pocket.

"Bird brain," I angrily insulted him and stalked toward the front of the bus. I poked the obese man in row seven. He did not stir. "Fried chicken," I shouted.

"Where, where?" As I expected, he became alert.

"Right outside the bus. I can smell it. Quick, go get it," I urged.

The large man tried to stand, his abdomen becoming wedged between his own seat and the seat in front of him. He wiggled and jiggled and twisted and turned, finally achieving an upright position. "I don't see any chicken," he wailed.

"Outside. Go. Go."

"There's no chicken. I know there isn't," he sniveled and plopped back down. His lips were smacking the air as if trying to taste some invisible food.

This man infuriated me. He seemed large enough to break down the door, and I wanted him to do so. "I'm going to eat the chicken all by myself."

"You can't do that."

"You bet I will." I began to march toward the front of the bus. Struggling and panting, he managed to stand back up and tottered into the aisle. As I turned around, I witnessed him fall sideways back onto his seat. An alarm-like noise sounded, and a flashing light up front caught my attention.

The dashboard screen was displaying a message. I cautiously moved close enough to read the word "Transfer" flashing repeatedly across it. The button with seat number 7 was also lit up.

The alarm sound persisted, shrill in my ears, likely correlated to the flashing screen. No one stirred. No one got up to investigate. *Peas of the same pod,* I thought to myself.

The ruckus began to hurt my ears. Having no alternative, I slammed my palm on the number 7 button and whirled around. The obese man, lopsided over his seat, was turning green as his seat was shaking violently. "Help," he screamed. I had no idea what to do. He was too large to move to another seat. The seat kept rocking and swaying; he remained mostly horizontal. The alarm continued. "Transfer" repeatedly flashed on the dashboard screen.

Maybe he's got to go, I considered. Scanning the other buttons, I caught sight of a button I had not noticed previously--an eject button. I briefly hesitated, and then I pressed it with determination. The big guy shot up as the ceiling of the bus opened. In an instant, he was gone. The alarm noise ceased. No one seemed to have been the least bit concerned about what had transpired. I had a suspicion that the man transferred to the ship, but who knew how much weight the ship could handle?

Small objects rained down and hit my head while the ceiling of the bus closed. I picked one up and identified it as a piece of candy. The candy must have fallen out of the man's pockets.

I found myself settling into the driver's seat. If I wasn't so painfully aware of my predicament, I might have enjoyed sitting at the controls of a large bus, especially since I was too young to even drive a car.

Another alarm sounded. Can't a guy get a rest? The screen flashed a new message that looked like an address. 2814 N. Wood. I didn't have a clue as to the location of that address or how to drive when one can't see out the windshield.

To my dismay, the alarm's volume began increasing. I could not find a volume switch anywhere. I banged on the screen. No effect. How I wished for a hammer to destroy the annoying screen!

Then I realized something: Just like my mother was picked up, maybe someone on Wood Street needed a pickup. A good-for-nothing like all the others, I presumed. The driver was missing in action. No one was available for pickups. Was I expected to do the pickups, or should I endeavor to find the driver?

Even if I knew how to drive, driving this bus through a haze was equivalent to driving with your eyes closed. Suicidal. The only option was to find the crazy driver who probably possessed the special skills required to steer a bus without being able to see a road, but how should I go about finding him?

I would utilize the easiest method first--calling. "Driver? Driver? There's a pickup. Anyone know where the driver is?" No one answered me. I decided to test the imbeciles on board. "I smell smoke. Fire!" I shouted over the alarm. No one stirred.

Could the driver still be on the bus? It couldn't hurt to check. First, I passed the birdman. His finger was excitedly tapping an image of some bird on his phone screen. His magazine was open on the next seat, displaying all kinds of bird nests. I shuddered as I passed the enormous man's empty and intact seat. No trace of his former existence remained, almost as if he had never existed. The alarm spontaneously stopped, but other unpleasant noises awaited me.

Trudy, the heavier of the two gossiping women, was ushering me over. "So what happened to Flint? I follow Ann on her Facebook page, but I can't find Flint. He must have some online presence."

"Yeah, who is he with now?" piped the second woman named Florence. "That Ann...She definitely didn't help Flint settle down *at all* if you know what I mean."

"Flint is at sea," I offered as a warning, "and

you guys are going to join him if you don't watch it."

"What does that mean?" innocently asked Florence.

"You should do positive things with your life and stop gossiping day and night."

"Well, I have never been so insulted by a little twerp," cried Florence.

"Remember Paula's son? He reminds me of him...sharp with his words," added Trudy. "Took after his mother and not in a good way."

"Like Daisy and her mother," quipped Florence.

I was curious, so I returned to the dashboard and examined the rows of numbers to the left of the driver's seat. The seat numbers of the gossiping women were 14 and 15. My fingers lightly touched the corresponding buttons. Then, I pressed harder, and to my satisfaction, the seat numbers lit up. I looked back over my shoulder to reassure myself of my decision. The women were indeed pathetic, their mouths still moving. My finger hovered over the eject button, tempted by the prospect of ridding myself of their incessant chatter. I pressed it and whirled around. "Safe trip." I smirked as the two women shot out through the roof screaming.

"Row, row, row your boat gently down the stream. Talking, talking, talking, talking, making everyone want to scream," I sang and then felt a bit guilty.

Less than a minute later, I heard the sounds of bird calls coming from the birdman's phone. The women's incessant chatter had likely drowned out the noise from his phone; now it was clearly audible.

I charged over to the birdman. "Did you see what happened?"

"Beautiful bird call isn't it? One of my favorites," replied the birdman.

"Don't you ever have plans, goals, things like that?"

"Ever see a bird nest that looks like a bale of hay? It can hold up to 400 sociable weavers."

"Birds are a hobby. You are a person, and you need a purpose in life," I lectured to deaf ears. "Your time is coming. I'm warning you."

The alarm sounded again. Rats. The screen was flashing that same address on Wood Street again. I had to face the facts: I was the new driver. I sat down at the steering wheel, fastened the seat belt, and shifted the bus into drive. Immediately, the alarm ceased. The windshield remained cloudy. Firmly closing my eyes in fear and dread, I pressed the gas pedal lightly. The bus lurched, and I felt forward movement.

Opening my eyes, I noticed that the windshield had cleared. I was driving! Thank goodness, I didn't see any traffic because I didn't want to crash into anyone. There was no road or street lights, but there was a sort of white path. My hands adjusted the steering wheel slightly to keep the bus moving along the white path.

Now, how to get to 2814 N. Wood? I had absolutely no idea. I kept steering along the white path. The drive was pretty quiet. I couldn't help myself. I pressed the horn for the novelty of it and took a peek over my shoulder. No one seemed to mind.

The path curved toward the right, a welcome change from the endless straight white road. A few minutes later, I began to see cars, streets, houses, and even a pedestrian.

"Game over," I announced to myself and pressed the brake. Without a license, I was not going to drive a bus on a real street and possibly kill someone and have the cops arrest me and haul me to jail.

The brakes did not work. I panicked and pushed my foot harder. Sweat dripped from my forehead. The address kept flashing on the screen above the dashboard. Looking out the windshield, I noticed the address numbers were decreasing: 2840. 2838. Soon, I'd be at the house. 2818. 2816. 2814. I pressed the brake again and sighed loudly as the bus rolled to a stop.

Without consideration or reservation, I jumped out of the seat and ran at the door. The door wouldn't budge. Through the glass panel, I could clearly read the address of the house. The window curtain of the front room momentarily parted before the front door of the house opened. A middle-aged man dressed in a suit and carrying a briefcase emerged and headed toward the bus. He reached the door and knocked.

"Open the door. Now."

I startled and whirled around. The voice was coming from the bus driver, yelling orders at me from the ceiling. Scared, I scuttled back up the steps to the driver's seat to push the door lever to enable the man's entry, precluding my own escape.

"Sorry for the delay, sir," I apologized as the man entered.

"Not sir. Professor Baumgartner to you."

"With that ego, I can see why you were picked up by the bus, buddy."

"PROFESSOR. NOT BUDDY."

"Don't think you are going to be distinguished in any way on this bus."

"I will be shown the respect that I deserve. I have a PhD in xenology in advanced research methods for the study of alien cultures and habitats."

"Meaning you are useless to society. Thought so."

"I have many articles published in scientific journals."

"Just have a seat, man. I happen to know way more about this bus game than you do, and you'd be smart to be quiet and figure out how to better contribute to society."

Scowling and huffing, the professor (although I don't feel he is worthy of any title of respect) hurried to a seat. Apparently, the idiot thought he was being picked up for a seminar.

The driver had disappeared; the houses and roads were no longer visible as the windshield clouded over once again. I contemplated my options. Great, the professor was ambling back over to me.

"I would like to see your driver's license," he stated.

"Don't have one." I smiled, enjoying his expression of disdain. "I'm only thirteen."

"Get out of that seat at once," he ordered. "I demand a licensed driver."

"No problem." I happily jumped out of the seat.

"Who will drive?" the professor whined. "I must be present at the seminar."

I shrugged and began walking away from him.

"I'm going to be late," he whimpered. He didn't even take note of the clouded windshield. In an instant, he was at the birdman's side. "Drive," he commanded.

"Can you name the fastest flying bird?" the birdman quizzed. "I can." He paused as the professor stared incredulously. "The peregrine falcon can reach speeds up to 240 miles per hour diving."

"I am a professor with a PhD in xenology. This is beneath me. Drive the bus at once."

"I'm not a bus driver. In fact, I rarely drive at all. I prefer to go by foot and study birds with my binoculars."

"What a pity to be crazy as a loon," mocked the professor.

"Enough," I declared, approaching the professor. I stared directly into his bespectacled eyes. "Either you find a seat or I'll send you into oblivion and beyond, and there are no seminars up there," I threatened.

The professor remained standing in defiance. "Put your pen on this seat," I ordered, pointing at a vacant seat, "and don't touch it." I walked to the dashboard and promptly ejected the pen through the roof.

"But that was my expensive pen," cried the professor.

"Sit down, or I'll eject you too. I mean it."

He immediately found a seat without further protest. I was almost beginning to enjoy being on the bus. I think the birdman missed the entire episode, his head buried in his feathers or maybe in a magazine.

"Anyone know a faster route to get downtown?" called out the professor.

Not surprisingly, no one answered. The birdman remained preoccupied. The teenage gamer either didn't care or didn't hear. The professor began having a fit. Like the others, I learned to drown him out.

CHAPTER TEN

Scott woke up tired, having tossed and turned to avoid the dog for most of the night. Sherry was still asleep. As Scott rose from the bed, the dog curled up against his pillow, and he resisted kicking it.

"This is my pillow, my bed, my house, mine, mine, mine, not yours," he rebuked the dog and then felt foolish. A better game plan would be to drop the dog off at an animal shelter and be rid of it.

Coffee would help too, a nice, fresh hot cup, thought Scott. The coffee would energize him in his search for Danny, and later, he could dispose of the dog. He sensed something was off as Danny's friends, Sara and Eric, did not seem the least bit surprised by Danny's disappearance and acted only mildly concerned. He would probe them and then probe them further until they revealed Danny's whereabouts.

Scott found the homeless man munching happily in the kitchen. Before he could express his displeasure, he thought he caught a glimpse of Officer Miller roaming around the backyard through the kitchen window. Quickly, he exited the backdoor and argued with the officer.

"If Danny were in the yard, don't you think he would enter the house? Don't you think you should concentrate your efforts on bus stops?"

"There is no bus stop where your son disappeared. Remember?" the officer retorted with annoyance. "Just looking around. That's all."

"Whatever." Scott didn't have the patience to argue while his house was still overrun by strangers. He reentered the house. "Get your fingers out of there!"

The homeless man was licking his fingers and returning them to the cookie jar, completely disregarding Scott. In a fit of rage, Scott forcefully removed the man's hand.

"Get out." Scott held open the back door. The homeless man lifted the bottom of his t-shirt to wipe his face and left without a word. Scott smiled. "One down." He locked the back door.

As Scott tidied the kitchen, he heard a knock at the front door. "Now what?" he grumbled as he walked to the door and cracked it open. The homeless man thrust his foot into the door opening. "No you don't. You are not coming back inside."

Officer Miller was standing behind him on the front stoop. "Yes he is. Let him in. I have some questions for him."

Scott shook his head in frustration as the homeless man reentered. Meanwhile, Sherry whizzed by clutching her purse and a file. "Client to meet."

"But Danny..." Scott started to protest. Sherry was already out the door.

The homeless man beelined to the kitchen, eyeing the cookie jar. By the time the officer got to the kitchen, he had two cookies in his mouth.

"You need to pay attention and answer my questions," ordered the officer.

Instead, the homeless man opened the refrigerator and poured himself a glass of milk.

"Answer me this instant. Did you see a thirteen-year old boy throughout your time at this hotel--I mean house?"

The homeless man was now opening cabinets. Officer Miller jingled handcuffs in front of his face.

"OK. OK. What did you ask me?"

"Did you see a young boy around here or not?"

"I saw a lady looking mighty fine in her exercise clothes. Do you want me to describe her to you?"

"NO! I asked about a young boy."

"Why would I be looking for him when the pretty lady is walking around?"

Officer Miller fingered his club, imagining clobbering the homeless man to calm himself down. He recalled another guy having been around the house and called Scott's name.

The sleeping outline of Trent on the living room couch had caught Scott's attention when he begrudgingly let the homeless man back in with the officer. "Get up, you lazy idiot. Don't you have a job to get to?"

"Nope," Trent replied groggily. "Laid off a while back."

"You mean fired, I bet," challenged Scott.

"I don't like word games," retorted Trent.

"Get out of MY house and start looking for work."

"Not today."

"Then you don't eat today. Suit yourself." Scott threatened, pointing to the front door.

"I need a shower," Trent said earnestly.

Officer Miller was shouting something from the kitchen. Scott walked over there to better hear him. "Don't lose sight of the guy in the living room. I have a few more questions for him."

"Officer, you don't understand..." Scott pleaded.

"No, Mr. Lewis, you don't understand. You lost your son and are simply impeding any sort of investigation."

"What do these crazy people have to do with Danny? I want my privacy. You're practically demanding me to leave my front door open and have some sort of homeless shelter for the deranged? This is absurd."

"If you let me do my job, I can figure out

what these people have to do with the disappearance of your son."

"I'll tell you what they have to do with Danny. Absolutely nothing. There, your job is done. Now get them out of here. Please."

Officer Miller rolled his eyes, ignoring Scott's comments. "Isn't there one more?"

"The dog?" Scott asked incredulously.

"No, the young kid." The officer had to stop himself from yelling, "No, the young kid, you idiot."

"I forgot about him," Scott admitted and marched angrily into Danny's room. He found the teenager sleeping and shook him. "Get up. You need to get ready for school."

"I don't go to school." The boy's eyes were fluttering to become alert.

"Give me your dad's number."

"Told you Dad's a drunk. He can't make it home from the bar half the time."

"Then your mom's number."

"She don't care about me."

"Ever meet a truant officer?"

"Sure. Many times. They always get a headache after they deal with me. One even changed jobs."

Feeling a headache coming on myself, thought Scott. "So what exactly do you do with yourself?"

"Whatever I want."

"That's a code word for nothing. You will amount to nothing. The officer wants to speak with you in the living room. Then you need to leave. You are not going to stay under my roof in my son's bed and do *whatever you want*, which means smooching off my money and eating my food."

Officer Miller grilled the teenager for no more than two minutes and abruptly put his papers away.

"What do you have?" eagerly inquired Scott.

"No more than last night. Sorry, pal."

"I advised you to keep investigating the transit authority and not waste time with these imbeciles. Can you at least get them out of my house for me?"

"This is not a police matter. You let them in; you let them out."

"I absolutely did not let them in," Scott vehemently denied.

"Then how did they get in, smartie? Pick the locks? Walk through closed doors? Did they crawl in through the windows?"

"I don't know how they all got here." Scott was seething at the officer's sarcasm. "I don't know any of them."

"Try holding the door open and maybe they'll leave," laughed the officer and promptly left the premises.

Had he not been an officer of the law, Scott would have punched him. "Mom," he cried into his phone. "My life is falling apart, and Danny is gone."

His mother was greatly disturbed, requesting to be picked up at once to assist him.

CHAPTER ELEVEN
(ON THE BUS)

"Your screen is blinking." The professor was lightly poking me with his index finger. I jumped. The alarm was beginning to sound as well. Apparently, I had dozed off. I was losing all sense of time, unaware of the day of the week or time of day. My watch had also stopped working.

Seeing my own address flashing on the screen caused my heart to begin racing. Not my mother! Please don't be a pick up for my mother, but for whom else could it be?

"I believe you need to tend to these computer issues immediately. They are delaying my arrival at the seminar," the professor insisted.

While contemplating my response, I heard bird sounds in the background despite the noise of the alarm. "I don't belong here with you loonies. You know that, don't you?" I lectured the professor.

"Get me to the seminar. I am introducing the guest speaker."

"You know what, pal? I think your seminar is long over by now, and I doubt anyone noticed you were absent."

"Do you know who I am?" glowered the professor.

"Certainly. A nutty professor who finally got what he deserved."

"How dare you insult my credentials."

"Look around, buddy. You were placed with a birdman, two gossiping dimwits, a fat pig, and a..."

"I will never ride this bus again," threatened the professor. "I will find another bus service that respects riders, and I will report you."

"Don't worry, sir. You'll be sailing around the world very soon and won't be near land to take any more buses."

"You need to be examined by a professional. You are speaking absurdities."

"I wasn't picked up by the bus. I voluntarily boarded by myself to rescue someone else. You were picked up by the bus because you belong on it, so who's the crazy one? Tell me professor. I asked you: Who is the mental case?"

As we argued, the alarm's volume increased to the point that conversation became nearly impossible. My own address, 7855 W. Courtland, remained flashing on the screen. The bus driver appeared on the ceiling.

"Not picking my mom up. Sorry fellow."

In response to my threat, the driver stared at me without speaking. The screen relentlessly flashed my address.

I suggested to the driver, "Might as well turn

it off. Not going there, no way, no how."

Expressionless, the driver remained fixed on the ceiling, constantly watching me. I looked away.

"Two can play this game," I taunted.

The bus lurched. The windshield cleared with houses appearing in plain view as well as children walking on the sidewalk. The bus swerved off the center of the road toward them.

"Are you crazy?" Instinctively, I grabbed the steering wheel, the bus narrowly missing the curb. A car honked angrily. I could not let go of the wheel lest the bus drive erratically and hit one of the children. Bird sounds, again, caught my attention. I hoped I would remain sane. Thankfully, the nutty professor had returned to his seat. Through the mirror, I watched him tapping his watch and muttering to himself.

Soon, the bus reached my block even though I had not paid attention to the direction or recognized the roads, fixating merely on not crashing the bus into any obstacles. I pressed hard on the brake. No luck. The bus continued toward my house. The driver's eyes, nearly hidden below the visor of his cap, were fixed on me. I shrugged at him, unwilling to assist in any manner in picking up my own mother, my hands firmly gripping the wheel and staying away from the door lever.

"Oh!" I exclaimed as my hand was involuntarily pushed to the door lever and a boy my age emerged from the front door of my house. He headed toward the bus. "Who is he?" I wondered. He boarded the bus, and the door closed. I was confused and bewildered. At least my mother was nowhere in sight.

Looking at my house, I glimpsed Dad's face at the window. He seemed pleased. "Dad!" I called as loudly as I could. Too late; the bus lurched forward.

"He can pay the fare for me," the kid declared, pointing at the professor and continuing down the aisle.

He had distracted my attention from my father. By the time I looked back outside, the windshield was clouded over.

"Wait, come back," I called to the kid.

He turned around to protest. "I already said I'm not paying. Want to arrest my parents? My dad's a drunk, and my mom's a party girl."

I left the driver's seat to face the boy. The driver had disappeared. The bus seemed to be able to navigate through the clouds or wherever we were by itself. "I couldn't care less about collecting fares for this bus if there are any. I want to know what you were doing in my house."

"Needed food and a bed. Didn't know it was your house, man."

"Do you know my parents?" I asked incredulously.

"If the man in the house is your dad, no. What's your issue?"

"So you just go into a stranger's house?" I

began to recall something. "Wait, were you on the bus with my mother?" I had remembered seeing a boy my age run off.

"If the lady in the house was your mother, I saw her very briefly. She's always going somewhere. I think I remember seeing her on a bus doing jumping jacks in the aisle."

"But you're back, and she's not."

"I don't know what you are talking about," complained the boy.

"I want to know why you are back on the bus and my mother is not. Does that mean she's safe?"

"Safe? Like are we playing some preschool game of tag and your house is safety? Or maybe zombies are chasing your mom. You have mental problems."

"I'm going to tell you what I told the nutty professor. I wasn't picked up by the bus. I voluntarily got on. You were picked up, so who's the crazy one now?"

"Just leave me alone, man. I couldn't get much sleep last night with that blasted, loudly-ticking clock. I finally took a hammer to it."

"Grandpa Lewis gave me the clock. It's an antique," I wailed.

"Oh well. A guy's gotta do what a guy's gotta do."

"Tell me you didn't smash my clock."

"I did you a favor. Can't get no sleep with that thing ticking all night."

"How dare you break my grandpa's clock."

"Next, I'll break your neck."   The kid showed me a fist.

I looked around helplessly for a weapon. The bus driver in the dark uniform appeared on the ceiling and shouted, "To your seats," with an expression of absolute displeasure.   Needless to say, we instantly separated without a word.

Relief that Mom was safe was short-lived. Again, my own address flashed on the screen.   To my further dismay, the professor was back out of his seat and heading in my direction.

"I will not tolerate that buffoon any longer. The bird noises must cease immediately."   The professor was pointing adamantly at the birdman.

"There's a reason you're both on the same bus. Bet you didn't think of that, PhD man."

"Make him stop, or get him off the bus.   No more word games."

"Must I spell things out for you?   I thought you have an advanced degree."   He stared at me dumbly.   "You and the birdman are equals. Equally useless."   I laughed light-heartedly until the alarm changed my mood.   I would have to drive to my house and pick up my own mother. "Sit down, or I'll do to you what I did to your pen," I warned and pointed at the ceiling.

"No, no."   The professor ran back to his seat like an obedient, young child.

CHAPTER TWELVE

"Mother, quick!" Scott beckoned her to the living room window, but it was too late. The gray bus had disappeared.

"What's wrong, Scott?" his mother inquired in a genuinely concerned voice.

"I saw the strangest sight. This gray bus, hazy-like, picked up that good-for-nothing, lazy teenager and practically vanished into thin air. The bus was almost unearthly."

"Wow." Mrs. Lewis, normally able to access an array of words, could express nothing else at the moment.

At noon-time, Scott found the homeless man poking around his closet, one of his dress shirts draped over the man's back. "That's my nice work shirt, which you don't have a use for." Scott yanked the shirt off him. "I don't care if you don't own a cent. Taking my shirt without permission is stealing. And why don't you have manners? Does a lack of money give you the right to act like an animal? This shirt should suffice for your occupation." Scott threw a T-shirt and a pair of sweatpants at him. "Go change in the bathroom. Get out of my bedroom."

Scott proceeded to the kitchen. Two empty bottles of liquor--two expensive bottles of liquor that Scott had been saving for a momentous occasion--were strewn on the floor. "Useless human being," Scott muttered angrily.

The dog entered the kitchen with pleading eyes. "Where do you normally eat? This isn't your house." Of course, the dog could not answer, continuing to plead with its eyes. "I don't have any dog food." Scott tossed a bun at the dog, and the dog gulped it down. "Wait a minute. You didn't bark to go out this morning."

Scott suddenly felt uneasy. He had a bad feeling as he raced down the basement steps to inspect his work table where the dog had spent the night. He cussed, finding a pile of dog poop under his work area. "Useless dog. I'm not going to feed it one more crumb." Begrudgingly, Scott cleaned the mess and sprayed air freshener all around the room. He returned upstairs to find the dog asleep on his recliner, fighting the urge to kick it off.

He looked out the living room window, mentally planning a route to search for Danny. The homeless man headed out the door without a word of thanks. For no apparent reason, the dog startled and ran out with him.

"Wonderful, finally a stroke of good luck." Scott quickly locked the door after them and returned to the window to watch where they were headed. The gray bus appeared. Both the homeless man and the Lhasa apso boarded. Instantaneously, the bus disintegrated before Scott's eyes, gone without a trace. Scott stood staring absently, trying to process what had transpired.

Mrs. Lewis entered through the back door, having visited the next-door neighbor.

"Mother, please come here," Scott called urgently.

"Yes, what is it?" Mrs. Lewis practically sprinted into the room.

"I saw that gray bus again. You know, Danny kept asking me about buses, and I didn't understand why. Then, Sherry disappears and Danny claims she's with Flint, and I couldn't figure out how he would know that. Sherry suddenly reappears from some bus out of nowhere that no one can identify, including the police. Next, Danny disappears and his friends say he boarded a gray bus. Now, I keep seeing this strange gray bus like no other. I can't make any sense of it all, but the stories seem connected. I strongly believe I need to figure out where this bus goes to get to Danny."

"To think that Sherry got off and Danny got on, but how? Why?" Mrs. Lewis mused aloud.

"What are you saying, Mother?"

"I'm so sorry, Scott, but I have no explanations for things I don't understand much more than you do."

"Mother, is Danny on that bus? Answer me." Scott was becoming increasingly frustrated, sensing his mother knew more than he did.

Mrs. Lewis took a moment to contemplate

before responding. "Very possibly but…"

"Give me the name of the bus company now." Scott removed his cell phone from his pants pocket.

"It's not like that, Scott…"

"I want the name of the company," Scott repeated firmly.

"I don't believe there is a name, and I certainly don't have it." Mrs. Lewis was close to tears.

"You leave me no choice, Mother. Either the police will get the name of the company out of you, or they'll get it out of Danny's friends, but they're going to get it." Scott began dialing.

Mrs. Lewis yanked the phone away, shocking her son. She spoke quickly before he could protest. "You said the bus was unearthly, remember?" She now had her son's attention. "I think the bus is out of human control."

"No, Mother. I will not lose Danny and accept some irrational explanation. I'm going to hunt him down myself."

CHAPTER THIRTEEN
(ON THE BUS)

Visibility improved, but I closed my eyes as soon as I recognized my own block. I did not want my mother back on the bus. Unable to resist the urge, I peeked as the bus slowed to a stop and spotted my house. "Dad!" I waved frantically and leapt out of the driver's seat only to have my path blocked by an unkempt, homeless gentleman (dressed in clothes resembling my father's) and a dog that began boarding.

"Let me off." I tried to push the man out of my way. Too late. The bus lurched. The windows clouded over.

"You ruined everything. I couldn't get off," I yelled at the unkempt man.

He began singing and didn't sound like he ever had voice lessons. Despite feeling furious, I laughed as he went off key.

"Shut your mouth," demanded the professor. "I will not be disturbed from my studies." He stood up and glared at the homeless man, who began dancing in the aisle. The dog curled up on a seat and fell asleep.

With a look of utter disgust, the professor

walked up to the homeless man and hollered, "Get off the bus." He looked at me to assist in the effort. I shrugged. The homeless man grabbed the professor's hands and tried to twirl him in the narrow aisle.

The professor jerked his hands away. "I am presenting at a seminar today." He paused to straighten his suit jacket. "You will not touch me."

"Touched you, touched you," taunted the homeless man, poking the professor in the chest. Then, he skipped over to the birdman. "Touched you too, touched you too."

The birdman flapped his arms and nearly squawked at him. "Get away, get away."

"Don't go anywhere near me if you know what's good for you," warned the boy my age as the homeless proceeded down the aisle toward him. He displayed a fist to reinforce his message.

The homeless man leaped on to a seat and stood up tall, enjoying the attention. He flexed his fingers to resemble a microphone and began singing again.

"That's it. I'm calling the police. He's lost control," announced the professor and took out his cell phone.

As my own cell phone did not work on the bus, I was curious about what would occur when the professor attempted to make a call. To my surprise, he began conversing on the phone.

"There's a drunk and a buffoon disturbing

the peace," he complained. (I chortled.) "How? I'll tell you exactly how. By dancing and touching me without my permission and by playing loud bird noises. (I was actually able to hear a voice at the other end.) Yes, I said bird noises...No, I'm not outside...I should go inside if the birds are noisy? I AM INSIDE...You're asking if the bird noises are inside my head...(I burst out in laughter.) I AM A PROFESSOR WITH A PHD."

At this point, the birdman, teenage-phone-man, thirteen-year-old boy, and homeless man all shouted in unison, "QUIET!" Even the Lhasa apso perked up and barked three times.

"Sounds like you are the noisy one, sir," the lady on the line retorted and hung up.

For a while, the bus remained unusually quiet. Even the homeless man conked out. I was eager to question him about my house and my father. I tried my cell phone again, but there was no dial tone.

"Give me your phone or I'll eject you," I threatened the professor. He handed me his phone without protest. I prayed and dialed my father. The phone rang once. The phone rang twice. It rang a third time. I realized that my father wouldn't recognize the number. Unfortunately, the connection was lost. Upon further inspection, I noticed that the professor's mailbox was full. If I could somehow get through and leave a message for my dad, I wanted to be sure he would be able to leave me a message in case the professor was lost in his studies of aliens and didn't hear his phone ring. "Don't you ever delete any of your messages?" I scolded the professor.

"I am busy with research. I can't attend to petty problems," he replied.

"What if your mother needs to leave a message?" I challenged.

"I've clearly explained to her how important my research is."

"Your research is more important than your mother?! That's not too respectful."

The professor snorted. An alarm sounded, so I rushed over to investigate the dashboard. The word "Transfer" was flashing on the screen and seat number 26 was lit up. I smiled. By now, I knew the drill. "Happy sailing, buddy."

"I'll be late to the seminar," the professor cried as he sailed out through the roof of the bus.

The teenager with eyes glued to his phone came running up front. "Did I see a man go out the roof?" He seemed genuinely terrified.

"Yeah, you did," I told him frankly. "I didn't think you noticed anything that wasn't on your phone screen."

"That was pretty freaky." His voice rose in pitch.

"And he wasn't the first one. You couldn't have missed the big guy, the one who took up two seats," I responded. The teenager gave me a blank scare. "You're kidding me? How about the two women? Now that was entertaining. My own idea," I bragged. He showed no indication of recalling that incident either.

"People don't normally shoot through the roof of a bus. I don't like that."

"Normal people don't stare at their phone screen day and night."

"But I'm not harming anyone. You are literally ejecting people out through the roof of a moving bus," the teenage boy argued.

"You may not be harming anyone, but you are certainly not helping anyone. You are useless..." Uh oh. The alarm sounded. The teenager's seat, number 66, lit up. I looked at his face, and he panicked, suspecting trouble.

"Please don't do it to me. Take my phone away. I don't want it anymore. I promise I'll be better," the teenager begged me, close to tears.

The alarm continued to sound.

"Help me, please. I have a real plan on how to be better. I mean it." He was pleading and holding out his phone to me. I extended my hand and took the phone away from him. The alarm instantly ceased. The teenager rushed out the door and was gone. The bus moved on in a flash, leaving my mouth hanging open and my outstretched arm still holding the phone.

"He got off! He got off! Someone got off!" I was screaming in excitement. (Not surprisingly, no one else noticed the teenager getting off or heard my exclamations.) The question remained: How could I get off? I pressed the numbers on his phone screen for the sake of it. There was no dial tone.

CHAPTER FOURTEEN

Only one last stranger remained. Scott frowned, watching Trent lounging in his recliner chair in the living room, hoping the bus would come for him too. "Can you do something, anything constructive with your time?" he asked Trent.

"Didn't make plans today," Trent explained.

"Then I am going to make you choose between my plans. Plan A is you have five minutes to get off your bottom. Plan B is I help you get off your bottom. Plans C and D include me kicking your rear end."

"I got a plan," Trent announced gleefully. He picked up the telephone. "Pizza delivery, please-...extra cheese..."

Scott was seething. He would have to tend to Trent later because he did not wish to lose more time when he could be searching for Danny. He circled the park in his car for an hour and then increased the radius of his search. Danny would certainly have come home if he was in the area, Scott surmised. His friends had seen him board a bus. Maybe he was taken hostage. Or maybe he was on that unearthly bus. Should he return home and camp out by the front windows, waiting for the bus to return?

After a few more hours of driving around town, Scott returned home, disappointed and progressively becoming more anxious about his son's well-being. He listened to the messages on the answering machine, touched by a message from Sara sweetly inquiring if Danny had returned. (Sara had also attempted to call Danny in a séance without success.)

A news flash appeared on Scott's cell phone. A teenager missing for two years was found unharmed but amnestic of past events. "Danny better turn up today. I'm not waiting two more days, let alone two more years for a son of mine."

Sherry walked through the front door smiling. "Heard a wonderful story while I was on the treadmill..."

"I thought you had a meeting with a client."

"The meeting ended early. I missed the kick-boxing class by fifteen minutes, but I figured I could still make it to the gym before..."

Scott practically dragged his wife to their bedroom for privacy from Trent and slammed the door. "YOUR SON IS MISSING," he roared.

"I thought he got stuck on a bus."

"He doesn't take a bus to school. Remember?"

"I assumed it was a school trip."

"And when he didn't come home last night, what exactly did you assume?"

"The cop said all the people in the house scared him away, so I thought he went to Eric's," Sherry replied matter-of-factly.

"The crazy people that you brought into our home for reasons I cannot fathom had nothing to do with Danny's disappearance."

"I did no such thing, Scott," Sherry asserted defensively.

"I'm sorry, Sherry. In the beginning of our marriage, you were loving and caring, and then your work and exercise consumed you, taking over your life. I used to make up excuses, time after time, assuring myself things would get better and go back to how they used to be."

"What are you saying, Scott?" Sherry was beginning to realize her husband was deeply hurt.

"I am a grown man. If you fail me, I can pick up the pieces for a while. I can change my plans. Today, you failed our son. The irony is that you don't even know it. I don't want a woman who cares about herself more than her own son."

"I do love Danny," Sherry insisted. "You know I do."

"If you did, you would have been here. You can't have it both ways. Sorry, Sherry, you don't mean anything to me anymore. You have no place in this house."

"But I don't have the time to move right now, Scott. I have the new budget to work on--I'll probably need to hire help for that. Listen, what's important is that I love you and Danny with my whole heart. You know it to be true."

"This is not a normal relationship. Your constant exercise and never-ending business calls and meetings are useless to me. I bring in enough money that you don't need to be like that. You need to go, Sherry. I'll contact my lawyer."

"But I love you, Scott."

"Your kind of love is worthless." Scott abruptly turned and left the bedroom. Sherry threw herself down on the bed, bawling uncontrollably. Not before long, she received a call from a client and rushed to her office to arrange a meeting.

Scott returned to the bedroom to repose and think if he had made the right decision to divorce his wife of fifteen years. Yes, she was not the same woman he had married. He could not defend her precedence of work and exercise over family. In fact, he could hear her on a business call at that very moment. Immediately, he made a call to the police station, hoping for any news about Danny's whereabouts. There was none. Leaving the bedroom, Scott passed Sherry's office. Trent was seated next to her, crunching numbers.

"I got a job, big guy, working on a budget plan," Trent announced to Scott. "Are you happy now?"

"Working for my wife?" Scott asked in disgust.

"Got a problem with that?"

Scott thought for a moment. "Nope. You're

good for each other. I can assure you, however, that headquarters is moving very soon." He stalked to the living room in a fit of rage. His mother was reading on the sofa.

"Mother, I have something important to tell you." Scott's mood abruptly changed to melancholy. "I asked Sherry to leave. You know she's been unavailable lately and couldn't care less about Danny's disappearance."

Mrs. Lewis grabbed the sofa pillow beneath her bottom to prevent herself from jumping jubilantly. She clenched her teeth to avoid emitting a scream of delight. She tightened her core to prevent her body from performing a seated celebratory dance.

"Mother, did you hear me? You're not saying anything."

"Oh, I couldn't find the words for such a fateful decision. The turmoil you must have felt... The devastation you must presently feel."

"Yeah, you pretty much summed it up. Thank you for appreciating how difficult a decision this was, considering you have not always been supportive of Sherry."

Actually, Mrs. Lewis believed that the decision should not have been the least bit difficult. Her son should have chosen better from the beginning or thrown Sherry out soon after the wedding. In her opinion, Sherry had rapidly deteriorated, becoming more and more ill-suited for her son. "Maybe it's all for the best, Scott."

"How can you say such a thing?" Scott retorted bitterly.

"I saw signs that your marriage was in trouble."

"Of course you did. Just forget the whole thing. I need to figure out how to find Danny." Scott stared absently out the window and then began walking in circles.

CHAPTER FIFTEEN
(ON THE BUS)

"Don't be Mom. Please don't be Mom," I prayed as the bus, yet again, pulled up in front of my house.

Mom and a man whom I had never seen before emerged from my house. The man, slightly younger than Mom, looked pleased.

Dad's silhouette was visible near the front window. I frantically waved and called, but Dad did not turn around. I stood up from the driver's seat, descended the bus's steps and blocked the door. Mom and the unknown man were directly facing me. I could clearly see Mom's eyes through the glass of the door. She either did not recognize me or couldn't see me. "Run, Mom, run," I shouted. She continued waiting expectantly at the door without reaction.

The bus driver suddenly appeared behind me, startling me. I practically jumped. "Get off the bus," he barked.

He had caught me off guard. Did he say "Get off?" I could actually get off? Without a fight? No games? But wait. Mom would be getting on.

"Get off," he repeated. "You're not a passenger."

The choice was clear. Me or Mom. I couldn't have my mother board a bus full of loonies. "No," I refused. I aggressively shook my head to discourage my mother from boarding. Why couldn't she see me?

Dad rushed out the front door. He must have spotted the bus. He pushed the younger man out of his way to stand next to Mom. "Danny might be on there," I heard him tell her. He pounded on the bus door. "Danny, Danny, are you in there?" Apparently, Dad could not see me either even as I was standing right at the door.

"Get off the bus now," ordered the bus driver. He touched my back with a finger or something pointy with a round edge. I felt a burning sensation. "Ow." For a few seconds, I felt I might not be able to endure the pain. Still, I endeavored to ignore the pain and it gradually dissipated.

I felt another hot poker, this one almost piercing my spine. A moan escaped from my mouth, but then I clamped my teeth.

Mom was trying to pry the door open with her finger tips. Dad continued to pound the door and shout my name.

"If you are thinking about staying, don't think you will remain comfortable," warned the bus driver.

Another scalding sensation made me cringe. I looked longingly at Dad and the outside world, but Mom could potentially be locked up forever.

"Look below!" the bus driver bellowed. A trap door opened on the floor of the bus. A flash of a look was enough to make me cover my eyes. Rotting flesh and bones had been strewn in the area below. I felt like vomiting. By the time I reopened my eyes, the hideous image was thankfully gone.

Mom's face, the comforting face of my mother whom I had not seen for a long time, was pressed to the door, trying to peer inside. Then the face changed, desperate, unbecoming in nature, as the door continued to remain shut. The strange man inched closer, appearing undecided as to whether the door remaining closed was good or bad.

"Danny," shouted Dad. I waved to no avail. I longed to hug him.

The image of the bones resurfaced in my mind. Then other images: Mom's pleasant face, Mom's desperate face, Dad's look of longing. A scorching sensation was again building on my spine.

"Danny, I need you so badly," Dad called.

"I'll be late." Mom knocked on the bus door.

I bolted out the door without any resistance from the driver. Mom boarded without hesitation, not noticing me pass. Tears welled in my eyes. Mom would be gone forever. The strange man followed her up the stairs.

Arms enveloped me. The familiar scent of my father wafted to my nose. I sobbed uncontrollably, my head buried in Dad's chest. He stroked my hair. Suddenly, I jerked my head up. The bus was already gone. "Oh no, Mom..."

"Well, I finally have you back, Danny. Let's go into the house and talk. Maybe you can shed some light on Mom and that bus. I can't figure out any of it (*except that the whole bunch of them are nuts,* Scott thought to himself)."

Grandma greeted me at the door and pulled me toward her. She was overjoyed at seeing me, incessantly talking and possibly reciting some poetry that expressed her emotions.

"But Mom is gone," I interrupted.

Grandma gave Dad an askance look. We headed to the living room, and they both listened intently to the tale of my bus ride, including all of the details from the ejection of the gossiping ladies to the wacky birdman and arrogant professor.

"Sounds like the bus crowd is no loss to society," Grandma commented.

"Watch it. My ex is on there," threatened Scott.

"Ex, like ex-wife?" My voice rose an octave in panic. "You mean Mom?"

Dad placed his hands on my shoulders. I knew what that meant. He had gotten rid of Mom. In a way, I had too by choosing to get off the bus. "I understand, Dad, but shouldn't we still try to save her?"

"Of course, Danny. You may have more insight as to how to help her than we do."

"We'll all work together," Grandma assured, letting go of some of her resentment of Mom.

We talked a bit more, and then I excused myself to call my friends. They were absolutely thrilled to hear I was safely back home. We met at the ice cream parlor. Sara and Eric were so engrossed in my descriptions of the bus and its passengers that both of their ice creams began melting into a soupy mass.

"Bummer," Eric remarked. "So sorry your mom's back on the bus."

"And my parents are separating," I added sadly.

"We're really sorry about everything," Sara added sincerely. "But we'll help you get your mom back."

"How? Even you couldn't summon her, and Flint is on some ship and will likely be thrown overboard."

"Let me think. Who else can help? Oh, I know," piped in Eric. He began barking.

"You're nuts, man." I shook my head. Then Eric started whistling. People in the parlor turned to watch the spectacle; my face turned red. "Eric, we're in public."

"Don't you get it?" smiled Eric. "We'll summon someone else on the bus like the dog or the bird guy."

"Great idea. Got a picture of the dog for the summons?" I contested in a sarcastic tone.

Sara protested my satire. "He is definitely

on to something. There were others on the bus…
like the homeless guy and the spoiled kid."

"But no pictures," I reiterated.

"How about that guy that you saw following your mother?"

"No clue who he was."

"Why don't you ask your dad about him,"
urged Eric.

Dad recalled that the man's name was Trent.
A bit of research (mostly to the credit of Sara)
revealed a newspaper article regarding a missing
man named Trent Dowd with an enclosed photo
of him. We raced down to the basement at dusk to
summon him with the usual candle and photo.

"Trent Dowd, Trent Dowd," Sara chanted.

"Either you quit the bird calling or I'll chop
off your wings, you idiot," we heard a man's voice
saying.

"Trent Dowd," gently repeated Sara.

"And you smell, wild man. Ever take a
shower? Don't sit anywhere near me, you hear?
And lay off the liquor. I smell it on your breath."

"Trent," Sara now called firmly.

"What do you want from me? I don't recognize you. I don't have time for anyone other than
myself."

"Then he fits right in the bus crowd," I muttered to Eric, giggling.

"How dare you call me and laugh." Trent switched gears mid-thought. "Hey, how about a pizza delivery for me and a salad for the lady? Could you arrange that?" His tone had softened.

"The lady? Can you please have her speak with us?" Sara pleaded.

The lady. He must be referring to Mom. I anxiously awaited his answer as my heart pounded inside my chest.

"No can do. She's exercising, and then she's got work to do. About that pizza..."

"Tell her that Danny needs her, please." Sara's voice rose in pitch.

"Mom!" I was desperate and yelled for the sake of it, doubting she would hear me.

"I'm waving at the lady. She is signaling to me 'later.' Didn't I tell you that she is exercising?"

"On a bus! She's really messed up." Eric's truthful remarks caused my eyes to tear.

"Just shout out 'Danny needs you'," Sara ordered.

"If this Danny dude is anything like the clowns around here, she doesn't need him."

"Listen," Sara fumed. "First of all, Danny is no dude. He is her son. Second, in case you don't realize it, you are on a bus full of clowns because you are one too."

Eric pumped his fist at that comment. I lamented the fact that Mom was among them. The communication ended abruptly.

Sara sensed my frustration and looked into my eyes. "Trent was obviously not the best pick, but this is definitely not the end," she assured me. "I'm not giving up on trying to get your mom back. We'll reassess and make a new plan."

We returned upstairs for a late snack; Dad was sipping a can of soda.

"I've been doing the shopping now that Mom hasn't been around," Dad explained, "so I hope you'll find something acceptable."

"Let's see," I responded, opening the snack cabinet. No more whole wheat pretzels! No more fat-free corn chips! Normal snacks to choose from. "You're doing excellent. Great."

My friends also complimented Dad's choices.

"What do you guys do in the basement, anyway?" Dad innocently inquired. "And what do you think researching that man Trent will accomplish?"

"Help," I pleaded to my friends with my eyes. Dad would never believe in summons of dead or half-dead people, however you label the people on the bus.

"Just looking for common denominators," Sara jumped in to explain. "Trent seemed to have been unable to hold down a job and had no significant contributions to society, social groups, or church, quite like the others on the bus. No insult to your wife intended."

"Don't worry about that. She made poor

choices." Dad accepted Sara's explanation and excused himself to our relief.

"Oh, oh!" We heard loud wailing from the living room. We sprinted there, terrified of what we would find. The possibility of Grandma having a heart attack crossed my mind. Instead, we found Grandma pointing at a strange man; her mouth was wide open, but she was unable to speak. Dad observed silently from a distance, a look of contemplation on his face.

"Who is that, Grandma? Are you OK?" I nervously asked, staring at the man's sweater vest, a style I had not seen before.

"Oh my." Grandma could say nothing else.

"Dad, should we dial 911?" I couldn't understand why he was just standing there doing nothing.

"It's Flint," Dad answered matter-of-factly.

"Flint? We didn't call him. Is he real?" Sara and Eric were just as confused as I was.

"Mother, I'm back. Aren't you going to hug me?" Flint approached his mother, arms open wide.

"Of course I'm going to hug you and never let you go." Grandma regained her ability to speak and nearly tackled her son. "I didn't think I would ever see you again."

Following a long embrace, Uncle Flint let go of Grandma and then hugged Dad tightly. In comparison, Dad's arms loosely encircled his brother, Dad's face expressing a mix of joy and apprehension. Uncle Flint turned in my direction and looked directly at me. I cringed at what I thought would be next. I was mistaken. He did not address me in the former (almost mocking) "little man Danny," but simply as Danny. I followed Dad's lead, arms weakly surrounding my uncle's torso. Sara and Eric observed silently.

We all sat down and listened to Uncle Flint's tale. I barely recognized his present demeanor, respectful and serious, recalling him as an ill-mannered man.

"Throughout, I didn't once reflect on my situation. Didn't even concern myself with the well-being of my family, including my own mother. I'm so ashamed."

As Uncle Flint lowered his head, I doubted his identity. Dad shot me a look of reassurance.

"I was on a bus. One of my former high school buddies was on it too with a few party-type guys. We all talked and joked around, laughed and told stories. Cursed our bosses and families. We were on our own, care-free and loving it. Yeah, some of the others were annoying. This obese guy would fall asleep and snore louder than a truck. Just awful. We'd poke him and he couldn't feel it through all those fat layers. Then there was this well-dressed, filthy-rich guy. He would ask us, 'Do you know who I am?' 'Couldn't care less,' we would answer. He would proceed to tell us his title, the number of shares he owned in some stock, the cost of his Italian suit, and go on and on.

"'You're a first class jerk,' we'd fire back. Then we'd pull at his tie and rub our grimy hands all over his suit. He'd wail like a baby. It was so much fun. Then one day, he was gone. We turned around and poof--he had disappeared. Again, I never reflected even for a moment. Was I really any better than that stuck-up individual?"

Uncle Flint hung his head a second time. No one interrupted his story, patiently waiting for him to regain his composure. While Dad's face looked unconvinced, Grandma had been nodding sympathetically as my uncle spoke. I raised my eyebrows at the seemingly long and (maybe fake) dramatic pause.

My uncle's head shot back up and he continued. Grandma, sitting at his side, rubbed his back for encouragement. Eric coughed (purposely). Sara glanced over at me.

"You know my memories are already starting to get hazy. I remember my past much more clearly than my more recent bus trip. I'll make the rest of the story faster. Somehow, I transferred to a ship. Boy was I excited, anticipating a new adventure. I hung out with guys just like me in the beginning.

"Then, I began to take notice of the others. The obese guy, to my dismay, was back and snoring like a foghorn. The rich jerk was showing people his expensive watch. But what really got to me were the new people: two ladies who could not stop babbling for the life of them. I swear they'd be able to talk with duct tape over their mouths. And a professor of stupidity. He tried to throw me overboard because I told him his research was good for nothing, explaining to him that a chef can offer you a decent meal, a carpenter can build you a house, and a doctor can take away your pain, but he was just a pain in the butt. I asked him to list three ways he was helping humanity, and he couldn't even come up with one. He was always shoving me to get in front of me because he felt like he was more important.

"Then, it hit me. Not one person on the ship was worth beans. How come there were no good people on the ship? I began thinking about you, Mother, and you, Scott and Danny, and even about some of my former bosses. I had been the problem all along. I was no better than any of the clowns on the ship or the bus. I vowed to change then and there, and that is my plan. In fact, I already have a few employment ideas with time allotted on my schedule for family. So here I am."

By the end, Dad and I were convinced that Uncle Flint had really changed. Dad opened a bottle of champagne and let me and my friends have a small taste. After losing Mom, having another family member around felt nice, especially given the small size of my family.

Sara took me aside. "So your mom has to change and then she can come back. That's the key."

"Easier said than done" was my realistic response.

Uncle Flint ambled over to me with a slight look of concern. "Your mom's at work, right? Although it is kind of late."

"Do you remember our call?" I wished to test him.

Uncle Flint stared blankly. "Remember you told me that you had seen Mom exercising on the bus but that you were too busy talking to the guys on the ship to help me?"

"I'm so sorry about that. I can't remember. What are you saying though? Your mom's on the bus?"

"I'm afraid so."

"I didn't think she was anything like me," Uncle Flint admitted.

"She manifested her issues differently," Sara worded delicately.

"How about my brother? How's he taking it?"

Eric came to my side as we informed Uncle Flint of the divorce. Uncle Flint immediately went over to Dad and Grandma, who had been engrossed in a conversation.

"I'm going back on the bus," Uncle Flint announced to them. "I'm going to save Sherry."

"Oh no, you don't," warned Grandma. "Now that you're back, I'm not losing you again."

"Danny lost his mother for heaven's sake," Uncle Flint argued.

"Not much worse than losing a sock in the dryer."

"Mother!"

Despite my sadness at Mom's disappearance, I couldn't help laughing at Grandma's comment. Eric covered his mouth to prevent himself from erupting in hysterics, as Grandma hurried away to check on something in the oven.

"Do you really think you can get back on the bus? After all, the bus driver pretty much forced Danny off the bus," Sara reasoned. "And what's the point? It would be like gaining one and losing another. When Danny got on, his mother got off, and when she got on, he got off. You lose one person to the bus each time."

"How do you get on the bus again? I don't remember?" Uncle Flint questioned.

"I think they find you," Eric answered frankly. "Like a magnet to metal, the bus finds all the good-for-nothings." Eric instantly regretted the insult. My uncle gracefully dismissed it with a wave.

Uncle Flint reflected for a moment. "Danny, your friend said your mom had issues. Can you be more specific as to why your mom may have been taken away? She's not evil, as far as I can remember. Kind of busy all the time, that's all."

"Because she focused more on exercise and work than on her family. I hate to say it, but it's true."

Dad joined us and was listening to the

conversation, bitterly adding, "Correction, Danny. Work and exercise were her *only* focus."

After a lull in the discussion, Eric blurted, "Maybe Sara can try to call the bus driver."

"Yeah, please do it, Sara," I entreated.

"Couldn't hurt to try," Sara conceded.

Dad looked at us as if we were deranged. "You're going to call the bus driver? How do you do that? Even the police couldn't figure that out."

Grandma hurried in from the kitchen. "I won't have Flint or any of you making contact with the bus, assuming you can do such a thing."

I shot Eric a look of desperation.

"It's kind of a joke between us that Sara can call the bus driver on her cell phone. Just ignore our silliness. This all started late one night when we were all tired and we couldn't focus on our studies any longer, so we kind of made this all up," Eric explained.

I nodded approvingly at Eric. He consistently was able to think faster than me in a tough situation. He winked back.

Even Grandma and Dad were satisfied with Eric's explanation since the concept of communicating with the bus driver was ridiculous to them. Eventually, Dad went to tinker in the basement while Grandma retired for the night. Meanwhile, we lost no time arranging with Uncle Flint to meet us in the basement at 10:30, after Dad would customarily head back upstairs to his room to watch the late-night news. Sara's father begrudgingly allowed her to stay until 11:00 "just this one time" after she lied to him about having a large assignment for school.

CHAPTER SIXTEEN

We tiptoed to the basement to devise a plan. Summoning my mother was ruled out as a viable option, consistently failing to work. Trent, the only passenger known to us to have been on the bus with Mom, had not cooperated. Uncle Flint decided calling the bus driver, as Eric had suggested earlier, was the best idea. We felt we had nothing to lose.

The usual candle was lit, and Uncle Flint led the chanting of "Bus Driver, Bus Driver." Lacking an actual picture of the driver, we hoped our memories would suffice. Uncle Flint attempted to recall the driver's features, but his memory was murky. In contrast, I was clearly able to visualize the bus driver's blue cap nearly covering his eyes along with his dark uniform. The memory of the rotting flesh and bones momentarily resurfaced, causing me to shudder.

Silence. Nothing occurred. Uncle Flint looked around uncertainly. Sara motioned to be patient.

"Bus Driver, Bus Driver." Eric's voice rose to the level of Uncle Flint's during the incantations. I stared at Uncle Flint's face, which only vaguely resembled that of the man I remembered.

Darkness. Silence. Sara signaled with an index finger to wait a bit longer.

"Bus Driver, Bus Driver." I joined in chanting more loudly, praying the driver would not ignore all of us.

Silence. Sara gazed down at the floor. Uncle Flint appeared fascinated by the process. Eric jumped up from his seated position on the floor. "He's not answering. We need a plan B."

A hand reached at Eric from the ceiling and yanked his arm, rapidly pulling him upwards. Uncle Flint sprang up to grab Eric's feet. Sara flashed on the light to better face the enemy.

The hand was from an arm donned in a blue sleeve, the bus driver's.

I helped my uncle tug at Eric's feet. Eric moaned in mid-air as he was being pulled in opposite directions.

"Let him down this instant," Uncle Flint demanded.

"I came on official business. Either I pick up or I transfer. There's no other choice." The driver's face with the blue cap nearly covering his eyes was now visible on the ceiling.

"You can't pick up Eric because he's an important part of school and the community as well as my very close friend," Sara bravely argued. "Your bus is solely for losers."

"I will empty a seat. I've done it before, and I'll do it again."

I recalled the exodus of people when I had boarded the bus. "He's not kidding," I warned Sara.

"Help me, guys," Eric begged, still dangling uncomfortably from the ceiling by one arm.

A Lhasa apso bounded into the room and barked loudly. Dad came running down the stairs to investigate. Eric was no longer in sight.

Dad began barking orders. "Get this dog out of my house at once. I'm not dealing with it again. You hear me?"

I recognized the dog from the bus, and my heart sank. I feared the bus driver had indeed emptied the dog's seat for Eric. What would I tell Eric's dad?"

"I repeat. I demand that this dog be removed right now. Are you listening to me, Danny?"

I didn't hear a word of what he was saying since I was busy mouthing to Sara, "Eric's on the bus." Sara became a nervous wreck.

"Whose dog is it?" Uncle Flint innocently asked.

Dad's face turned bright red as the dog climbed onto his workbench. I felt sick to my stomach about Eric. Sara held back tears. Dad looked ready to explode while everyone ignored him.

"Uncle Flint, Eric's on the bus too," I sadly informed him.

"WHAT?" Dad bellowed. "I'm not calling Mr. Bayne at 11:00 at night to tell him that his son is taking an imaginary ride on gray, flying bus. I want an end to all of this craziness."

Normally, Dad tends to lose patience as the hour becomes later, but I had never seen him this worked up before. I didn't know what to say.

"Danny," Dad said firmly, expecting some type of response. I looked down. "Sara," Dad said more gently.

"Eric's gone, Mr. Lewis. We need to accept that fact," Sara replied.

Anger flashed across Dad's eyes. Uncle Flint began rubbing Dad's shoulder; Dad angrily pulled away from him. "I am not doing this with another man's son. I am not dealing with those cops again. And I never want to mention that gray bus again. Is that clear?"

"Should we tell Eric's dad that he is sleeping over by you?" Sara suggested, ignoring the irrational comments. "However, he may consider why Eric is not making the call himself."

"This has to end now!" Dad continued his tirade.

"Calling Eric's dad is only a stall tactic. In the meantime, we need a plan to get him back. For once, why can't everybody be at home, safe and sound?" Sara bitterly complained.

"I guess I made things worse yet again," Uncle Flint lamented, more to himself.

Dad abruptly went upstairs; we followed, afraid of what he might do. To make matters worse, Sara's father, Mr. Swan, arrived, banging on the door. He refused to take a seat in the living room, threatening Sara about a grounding (but I swear it sounded like he said a pounding), rambling about responsibility and consideration for the late hour, and lecturing Dad about proper parenting.

As Dad prepared to roar (based on his facial expression), the doorbell rang. Without waiting to be let in, Eric's father, Mr. Bayne, charged into the hallway, startling Grandma, who had been leaving her room in the process of donning a bathrobe over her lavender nightgown to investigate the commotion. He muttered a brief "sorry" to Grandma and stood directly facing Mr. Swan.

"It's kind of late for a school night, don't you think?"

Mr. Bayne was a lawyer, calm and sharp-witted but heavy on sarcasm. "I believe our children have school tomorrow. They don't have the same options as adults, such as coming in later to work if they don't have an early meeting with a client." He surveyed the room looking slightly uncomfortable before asking, "Where is Eric? I'm not interested in playing hide-and-seek at this late hour."

"Mr. Bayne," Dad began calmly. "You are not going to be very happy because I was infuriated when they tried to give me the same explanation when Danny disappeared."

"Don't you dare go there, Scott."

"I'm sorry to have to tell you, but they're

161

saying Eric's on the bus," Dad blurted out.

"Listen, Scott. I never figured out exactly what happened to your son. Eric tried selling me a bill of goods a few times. You know very well he was on no bus. And in case your engineering brain also took a ride on a bus, let me clearly explain something to you. The police NEVER FOUND A BUS. WHERE IS MY SON?"

I had never seen Eric's father lose his temper before. Usually, he patiently stares people down, especially Eric, until they surrender. I'd also surrender to him; his look is dangerous. Dad was at a loss for words.

"How could you let someone else's child disappear?" Mr. Swan demanded. "I thought my daughter was safe here."

"What do I do now, Scott?" continued Mr. Bayne. "The police can't help without clues. Should I sing, 'The wheels of the bus go round and round,' until my son comes home? What should I tell his mother?"

Uncle Flint interceded. "You guys need to calm down. The insults will not bring Eric back."

"Who are you? Do you manage the bus company?" ridiculed Mr. Bayne.

"Better than that. I was a passenger on the bus for seven years."

Dad breathed deeply, grateful for the momentary silence as the stunned fathers scrutinized Uncle Flint. Mr. Bayne recovered too quickly.

"Wonderful." Mr. Bayne grabbed Uncle

Flint's arm. "Let's go to the bus station right now."

Mr. Swan followed suit and yanked Uncle Flint's other arm.

Sara pulled at her father's shirt. "The bus doesn't work like that, Daddy."

Dad tried to separate the men from his brother. The situation was becoming ugly. I was afraid of a brawl.

Just then, Grandma entered the living room, having cautiously been monitoring the situation from the hallway. She spoke with authority, like a strict teacher to her classroom. "Gentleman, please take a seat, and we will all deal with the situation in a rational, adult-like manner." Remarkably, the grown men sat down one by one.

"May I speak, Grandma?" Sara politely requested.

"Go ahead."

"Mr. Bayne shook his head in disgust. "Sara, time is of the essence. In case you don't remember before you begin giving a speech about love and patience, I have a son missing."

"With all due respect, Daddy and Mr. Bayne, Danny and his uncle are the only two who have first-hand knowledge of the bus process and may be able to advise us how to proceed."

"Fine. Let them show me the purported station," yelled Mr. Bayne.

"Please be quiet, Mr. Bayne. Sara is still speaking," Grandma reprimanded.

Mr. Bayne opened his mouth to protest.

Grandma adamantly pointed her index finger at him, and he silenced himself.

"Here are the facts," Sara continued. "There is no station. There is no direct number. We were, however, able to summon the bus driver. The problem is that he began threatening and took Eric away. Believe me that we tried to rescue Eric with all of our might, but the driver overpowered us. We are not dealing with normal circumstances."

"How do you call the driver if there's no number?" challenged Mr. Bayne.

Sara looked at me uncomfortably. Everyone anxiously awaited her response. I indicated that I was unsure how to provide him with a satisfactory answer.

"By candlelight," Uncle Flint responded in a confident, authoritative tone. "Light of a single candle. And we need to call the bus driver back. That's what we must do."

Uncle Flint's suggestion seemed like a bad plan to me. I was afraid the bus driver might take someone else away.

"Nonsense. Utter nonsense," Mr. Swan scoffed. "Poppycock."

"Bunch of hooey," Mr. Bayne chimed in.

"Quiet," Grandma warned. "We are adults solving a complex problem in this room. Your insults are not helpful."

Once again, Grandma restored the calm. Sara didn't like the plan either--I could tell by her worried facial expression. Seconds later, her expression changed to that of determination.

"Give us ten minutes," Sara requested. "If everyone could just sit for ten more minutes. If we fail, you have permission to call the police, but I doubt the police will be of much help."

"That's all you get, young lady. Not a minute longer," Mr. Bayne begrudgingly conceded.

Sara ushered me and Uncle Flint to the basement. She surprised me with a change of plan. Instead of summoning the bus driver (a move deemed too risky), we agreed to summon Eric. I pulled up a picture of Eric on my phone. The candle was lit, and the process began.

Nothing happened. Could Eric be transferring? He didn't even belong on the bus in the first place. Still nothing. We feared the bus driver might reappear instead. Uncle Flint assumed a fighter's stance. Nothing happened.

"What does this mean?" I asked Sara.

"I wish I knew. I really don't know."

I looked at Uncle Flint; he merely shrugged.

Embarrassed, we slowly made our way back upstairs.

"So what time is the bus scheduled to arrive in your imaginations?" derided Mr. Bayne. "Eric's a smart kid. How did he get involved in your insanity?"

Sara and I looked down at the floor.

Realizing we had failed, Mr. Swan declared,

"That's it. If it were my child that was missing, I wouldn't wait one more minute to involve the police."

Mr. Bayne nodded and called the police.

Officer Miller was over within minutes. "Lose your kid again?" he asked my father.

"No, I have my son, no thanks to your department."

"My son is the one missing, and I demand that you dispatch the entire department, or I'll sue you for negligence and dereliction of duty and ten other charges. Don't doubt me."

"Sir, there's no need to threaten. I'm already on it," assured the officer, immediately calling headquarters.

Fidgeting with a button on his uniform, the officer looked nervous, and Dad took notice. "Say, where's your partner? Lose him?"

The officer's lips quivered and his forehead wrinkled, as if he might cry.

"Sorry," Dad apologized. "I didn't mean to be a jerk (although Dad had definitely meant to be a jerk). Is he sick or injured?"

"No, Moore was feeling fine, absolutely fine. He's just not around."

"Not around? So you threw his body into the lake!" Dad was getting back at the officer for suggesting he had done the same with his wife.

"Of course not. I'm an officer of the law."

"Then you lost him! Can't keep track of your own partner. No phone records. No credit card trails. Bummer." Dad began laughing hysterically. Mr. Swan, however, was not the least bit amused, never cracking a smile. He uttered "Idiots" under his breath.

"No such thing occurred," the officer defended. He continued to look on the verge of tears.

"Is he on the bus?" Sara was frightened by her own suggestion.

"Come on, Sara," reprimanded her father, "you're beginning to make a mockery of this entire situation. Soon, you'll have the whole city riding the bus."

Ignoring Mr. Swan, Officer Miller fumed. "So these kids do know something about the recent disappearances. I just knew it."

"Are you saying that these eighth-grade children have information that your incompetent department doesn't?" Dad glared at the officer.

"I implied no such thing."

"Can we stop focusing on this bus craziness so we can find Eric?" Mr. Swan hollered.

"Well, if he can't keep track of his own officers, how is he going to find my son?" bitterly added Mr. Bayne.

"I have already ordered our best officers to search the area. You have my word," Officer Miller assured.

"I am not even confident that you are capable of providing me a list of names assigned to the case. I'll arrange for my own private investigator. You're a pathetic excuse for a police officer." With that, Mr. Bayne stormed angrily out the door, bidding no one a good night. On the way to his car, he busily tapped at his phone screen.

"Let's go, Sara." Her father led her out the door without further comment.

Officer Miller also took his leave. I stood next to Dad, feeling awful. Dad's face displayed a mix of anger and sadness. Uncle Flint pouted.

"Everything will work out," Grandma promised, but we were unconvinced.

We sat in silence on the sofas in the living room. The time was well past midnight.

After much deliberation, I finally spoke. "I need to get back on the bus. It's all my fault that Eric is gone because I couldn't stop Mom..."

"No," Dad objected. "No, you had nothing to do with your mother's issues."

"Should never have married that woman," Grandma muttered under her breath.

"Mother," Dad scolded.

"If anyone goes back on the bus, it will be me," stated Uncle Flint.

Another lapse of silence.

"You should go to bed, Danny. It's late, and you have school tomorrow, actually today," Dad suggested, noting the time on his watch.

"Not with Eric missing. I refuse."

A knock sounded at the door.

"I don't want to let him in. I know that's terrible," Dad apologized to us as he stood up. "He's just being unreasonable--that Mr. Bayne." More knocking. "Fine, I'm coming." Dad was dragging his feet. "His sarcasm is just not the least bit helpful. Now what do you want?" Dad grumbled as he thrust open the door.

I ran full speed at the door, nearly tackling my dad. It was Eric! "How'd you get back? Your dad's an absolute mess."

"So glad to see you." Dad patted Eric's back. "I'm going to call your father right now. He is worried sick and ..." (Dad probably stopped himself mid-sentence from adding the words "obnoxious, a pain in the neck, and most disagreeable.")

"A miracle!" exclaimed Grandma.

"Danny's mom is not with you, is she?" Uncle Flint addressed Eric. Eric nodded no. "Too bad. That would have been something if she also came back."

"So how'd you get back, Eric?" I repeated.

"Believe it or not, the bus driver pulled up to the police station and that crazy officer--remember the rude, fat one--comes out biting into a sub sandwich, catsup smeared on his cheek. The door of the bus opened, must have been for him, and I ran off the bus as fast as lightning."

"I wonder why the others don't just run off the bus."

"They're all nuts. You know that, Danny. They really believe they are headed somewhere. I saw this girl--looked like a junior or senior in high school--she was so annoying, marching up and down the aisle reciting lines for some play she thought was going to make her famous. The bird-man that you told us about is still on the bus. He scolded the girl for drowning out his bird noises. And the man named Trent told her, 'Memorize this line: Everyone is tired of my babbling, so I'm just going to keep my mouth shut.' I couldn't help laughing."

"What about my mom?" I blurted. Despite his tough exterior, I caught Dad leaning forward, anxious to hear the answer.

"Well, finally, we had a little peace and quiet, but then your mom accidentally tumbled into the lap of the babbling, bobbling girl. The silence was broken and the girl began reciting a long string of curses and complaining that she could have been injured and her image permanently damaged, blah blah blah. Such an airhead."

"How did she tumble?" questioned Dad.

"She was doing some kind of balance thing in the aisle and lost it." Eric stood on one leg and raised the other leg out to the side. "Something like that."

Dad sighed.

"She can't stop, can she, Dad?" I sadly remarked to him.

"Did she mention Danny?" Dad addressed Eric, ignoring my comment.

"She wasn't really noticing me. I'm sorry."

The conversation was interrupted by the prompt arrival of Mr. Bayne. He warned Dad, "I don't know what's going on here but this is not happening again. You hear me?"

"Not under my control" was Dad's terse reply.

"I suggest you get some control of your life for the sake of everyone else."

"Mr. Bayne, the hour is late. Please just take your son home."

Eric, meanwhile, stealthily slipped me a small piece of paper. Uncle Flint had noticed. I read 9901 Benton, presumably an address. "What's there?" I whispered.

"Next stop on the bus, if you are interested. I saw it on the screen above the dashboard. Gotta go before my dad loses it."

As Eric was hustled out the door, I understood his brilliance. He had provided me another opportunity to rescue Mom.

Dad locked the front door and turned around. I stuffed the paper into my pocket. "Finally, the nightmare is over. Danny, please try to get some sleep."

Dad and Grandma wished me a good night and retired to their bedrooms. Uncle Flint approached me quietly. "What was that all about?"

I revealed the significance of Eric's message.

"Let me go there. I have nothing to lose," begged Uncle Flint.

"Grandma would never forgive me if she loses you again."

"Do you think she'll be any happier if she loses you?" he argued.

"I guess not." I thought for a moment. "OK, we'll both go. You back me up and pull me away if the driver tries to get me on again. I never wanted to see that bus again, but I gotta save Mom."

"Don't do it, Danny."

Uncle Flint failed to change my mind, so we devised a plan. I brushed my teeth and closed my bedroom door to feign sleep. Thirty minutes later, I tiptoed to the living room and met my uncle. We slipped out of the house.

As arranged by Uncle Flint, a car was waiting to pick us up.

"It's Lopez. He owes me one. Hop in."

We entered an old blue Cadillac; the driver immediately began conversing with my uncle. "Where you been, man? It's been like years, man."

"All in time, Lopez. First, I need this favor. Take us to 9901 Benton."

"What's over there?"

"Not sure, Lopez. We need to meet someone. You'll wait in the car. If I don't return, you take the kid back home, got it?"

"Got it man, but it's kinda late to be meeting folks."

"They don't keep normal hours, kind of like we used to be."

Lopez drove the remainder of the way to our destination in silence. I was feeling the lateness of the hour, praying that I would remain alert enough to rescue Mom. A worry surfaced. I had no idea what time the bus was coming. What if we arrived too late? Then, I remembered from my time on the bus that there was a significant gap in time from when the address appeared on the screen to when the pickup occurred. Maybe there was a chance we would catch the bus.

We arrived at the address and waited outside the car. Three minutes passed. Then five. My eyes began closing. Uncle Flint leaned in to support me, and I believe I fell asleep standing.

"Why don't you meet them in the morning?" Lopez shouted out the window. "You guys are like sleeping." I attempted to open my eyes, but the effort was too great.

Uncle Flint put an index finger over his lips. "Gotta keep your voice down, Lopez. We are waiting for a bus."

I kept my eyes closed.

"This ain't no bus stop, man."

"I know."

"So you're waiting for a bus where there ain't no stop."

"Something like that. This is a different kind of bus."

"You're loco, man."

"Just stay in the car, Lopez."

"Danny!" Uncle Flint called suddenly. I startled and opened my eyes. The gray bus had arrived. "When the door opens, stand in the doorway and call your mother loudly. I'm going to stand right behind you and hold my hands tightly around your waist. We'll take it from there."

"Now?" I was barely conscious.

"Wait," Uncle Flint ordered.

A scowling man emerged from the nearest house. "Move," he barked at us. "I'm getting on the bus and getting on now."

"I suggest you learn the word please and learn to be polite, or you're going to have a very long ride," chided Uncle Flint.

"Who do you think you are, telling me what to say and how to say it? And your vest is so old-fashioned. It looks like you haven't shopped in ten years."

"Insults will make your ride even longer."

"I'm not insulting, just saying what I see, and I see a…."

As the man prepared to swear, Uncle Flint blasted him. "Watch your language. My young nephew is standing here."

"So you like refined language. Then, let me educate him. Little boy, if you don't watch out, you're going to grow up to be a dunce, dingbat, dimwit, imbecile, and a blithering idiot just like your uncle. Like my vocabulary? Another time, I'm going to use more colorful words to describe you."

I think Uncle Flint was about to punch the guy when the bus sounded a horn. The guy shoved Uncle Flint aside to board the bus. Spotting the open door, I ascended the first step and called out, "Mom." Uncle Flint held me firmly as he had promised.

"Danny."

I heard her voice! How I craved her hug. "Yes, Mom, it's me."

"Oh, Danny, I want to see you, I'm just finishing my jumping jacks," she called, not even coming to the door.

"But Mom..."

I heard her breathing loudly from exertion. "Mom, the bus will leave. You need to get off NOW."

The door began closing. I blocked it with my body and hands with great difficulty. Uncle Flint continued to maintain a firm hold on my waist. "Mom, please come."

"Last ten," she panted. "Ten, nine..."

I was fighting fatigue to hold the door in the open position. I noticed the bus driver's evil grin and nearly lost my focus. The door was feeling heavier and heavier. My arms were aching.

"Six, five..."

"Mom, now or never, please!"

"Three, two..."

I couldn't hold out any longer. Uncle Flint jerked me backwards. The bus door completely closed. I pounded on it. "Mom!" I had lost her by one mere second.

Mom now appeared at the window of the door, a phone next to her ear. She signaled "one moment" with her index finger. Correction to my previous statement: I hadn't lost my mother, she had lost me. I cried into my uncle's sweater vest as the bus faded away.

Lopez drove us home. "So where does that bus go?" he innocently inquired.

"No place you want to go. Trust me, Lopez."

When we got home, we tiptoed into the house, and I collapsed on my bed. Uncle Flint assured me that in the morning, he would convince Dad to let me sleep until noon and attend school after lunch. I would have preferred to not go at all.

Sure enough, I woke up to a sunlit room. My replacement standard alarm clock displayed 11:52; the crazy boy on the bus had destroyed Grandpa Lewis's antique clock. At least I was no longer tired. I hurried while using the bathroom and threw on my clothes.

Hearing voices, I peeked into the living room. Officer Miller and another officer unfamiliar to me were speaking with Dad. Quickly, I retreated behind the wall. Too late. Dad had spotted me.

"Danny," Dad called. (Rats. Speaking with police officers was most stressful because they were always asking how somebody disappeared and they never liked the bus answer.) "The police have a few questions about Eric. You can understand that because the police were called to our house to look for Eric, and then he showed right back up here a little bit later. To be honest, I have a few questions myself."

"Chief Tucker, it's like I've been telling you," began Officer Miller. "This kid knows exactly what happened to Eric Bayne. You'll see."

"Tell the police exactly what happened to Eric, Danny. They need your account because he disappeared from our house. Officer Miller was unable to get enough details from Eric. Probably due to his trauma. As you can see, the chief is also here. This is very important."

"Everything's already been said," I protested.

"Just tell us what happened." Chief Tucker smiled at me. "That's all you need to do. No one is in trouble."

"The problem is that Eric's father won't believe what happened, so neither will you."

"Try us." Chief Tucker was almost succeeding in making me believe he was a friendly person.

"Don't let him weasel out of this one," hissed Officer Miller into the chief's ear.

Firmly believing the police were out to get me, my uneasiness returned. "Dad, they'll say I'm crazy and lock me up."

"You need to tell them something, Danny," Dad urged. "They'll believe you more than me."

"Flint's at the station cooperating for statements because he was also a missing person," explained Dad.

"But Dad..."

"He's up to no good, like I keep telling you, Tucker." Officer Miller was enjoying my anxiety. "The whole bunch of those kids are plotting..."

Ignoring Officer Miller, the chief continued

with a serious but not menacing tone. "Danny, we need a statement from you."

"There's no other way to say it," I stammered. "Eric was on the gray bus."

"You see!" Officer Miller jumped excitedly. "You can't get nothing out of them."

Feeling ashamed, I wished I could run away.

Chief Tucker paid no attention to Officer Miller. "Why didn't you just say so?"

"What?" I asked stupidly.

"What?" Officer Miller echoed more stupidly than me.

"All you needed to say was 'the gray bus.' No other explanation is necessary. Case closed." The chief grinned.

I did not respond. Maybe he was laying a trap, yet he looked so friendly.

"Gray bus my rear end. Threaten him," advised Officer Miller. "Threaten an arrest if he won't tell you the truth."

The chief continued. "Did a bus driver with a dark blue cap pick up Eric?"

Confused and discombobulated, all I could do was nod in the affirmative. The dog from the bus entered the room, curled up on the rug, and fell asleep.

"Not much I can do about him. It's not like I can arrest a dog," apologized the chief.

"My mother's still on the bus," I said ruefully.

"Yeah, I bet. The whole family is nuts,"

sneered Officer Miller.

"The bus driver is public enemy number one. I have a sketch and a file, but I think he's going to be a hard catch. The funny thing is that time goes by, and people seem to forget about the ones who disappear. I called a woman last week to apologize for a lack of leads on the disappearance of her teenage son who did abuse drugs, by the way. Believe it or not, she said, 'That's OK, my migraines have improved.' The gray bus...I have heard all about it."

"How'd you find out about it?" I never would have imagined asking this question of an officer of the law.

"Well, I had a friend, a smart fellow, and I lent him some money to start a business. I knew he'd make it big with his brains, and he did. The problem was that I never got my money back, and he was just too busy to meet me. And to him, the money that he owed me was like pennies, so he didn't care. One day, I went to his fancy office, and he was meeting with an important client in his fancy Italian suit and couldn't be bothered. Another day, he was being fitted for a tuxedo for some event. A third time, he was speaking to a king or a queen or a joker. Then, one day, he disappeared off the face of the earth. Nobody could tell me where he was. His secretary was really goofy about the whole deal, giving me stupid reasons, like he's on a long vacation.

"Being a detective, I was not going to let my

money go. I interviewed his staff and got nothing. I interviewed his brother, who also didn't know a thing. Finally, I spoke to his neighbor, who had witnessed him board a gray bus.

"This neighbor, you should know, was a computer programmer, like not a dummy. And he didn't drink, no alcohol ever. So if he claimed he had seen a gray bus, he had seen a gray bus. I began interviewing other people whose family members had suddenly disappeared without any motive or cause. Some of those people also mentioned having seen a gray bus. So just because I didn't see it, I have enough witnesses to establish credibility..."

Officer Miller went on a tirade. "And you believe all those crazy people?! What if they tell you they saw the Loch Ness Monster? You're just giving everyone a 'get out of jail free' card. They'll say they didn't do it because they were on the gray bus. Greatest alibi ever."

"That's quite enough, Miller. Our work is done here. Let's get going."

Not anticipating any future police interrogations, I felt a sense of relief.

Officer Miller remained standing in place, opening his mouth wide while mentally preparing his next argument. "I do believe we missed some crucial information, and if we leave, we may never know..."

Chief Tucker placed his palm on Officer Miller's back and pushed him towards the door, his legs stumbling forward. The lazy dog perked up and nipped Officer Miller's leg in the doorway. As the dog retreated, Dad patted its head affectionately.

"Ow, I didn't deserve that," cried Officer Miller, hobbling down the steps.

Chief Tucker peeked back through the doorway. "One last thing. Call me if any of you see Officer Moore around. I have my suspicions where he is."

I couldn't help myself, letting out a chuckle. If Sara was right and Officer Moore was on the gray bus, maybe he'd be the one to finally get Mom to sit down.

ACKNOWLEDGEMENTS

Thank you to my son, nieces, and nephews for listening to my stories for hours at end.

Thank you to all my patients for letting me entertain them while they exercised to make the recovery a bit easier.

To my parents for their endless support.

And to my husband for his constant encouragement.

My very special editor deserves heartfelt thanks for his many hours of editing and for ensuring the ideas flowed seamlessly.

Made in the USA
Monee, IL
24 November 2020